Pride Publishing books by Helena Stone:

Scenes from Adelaide Road

SCENES FROM ADELAIDE ROAD

HELENA STONE

Scenes from Adelaide Road
ISBN # 978-1-78430-905-3
©Copyright Helena Stone 2015
Cover Art by Posh Gosh ©Copyright December 2015
Interior text design by Claire Siemaszkiewicz
Pride Publishing

Published in 2015 by Pride Publishing, Newland House, The Point, Weaver Road, Lincoln, LN6 3QN, United Kingdom.

Pride Publishing is a subsidiary of Totally Entwined Group Limited.

SCENES FROM ADELAIDE ROAD

Dedication

For Tara. You've been a shining light and a source of inspiration since the day you were born. Thank you for everything and 'Anything'.

Chapter One

I took one step forward before retreating again. The wall against my back grounded me, taking some of my panic away. I stared across the street at the door, the bouncers and the slow trickle of people entering the club. I had waited for this moment, dreamed about it for months but now it had arrived I couldn't find the courage to take the last fifteen steps separating me from the threshold.

I forced myself to breathe slowly while I counted up to ten and down to zero again. My body was on high alert, thoughts rushed through my mind and worry cramped my stomach. This was ridiculous. I only wanted to enter a club, discover what it was like on the inside in order to satisfy my curiosity. Here in Dublin, I had no reason to be afraid — there was no one to tell me what I could and couldn't do, and, most importantly, nobody to frown upon me and who I was.

I was free at last, but I might as well still be shackled to my father and his rules for all the good it did me. I could hear the contemptuous words my dad used to spew at me whenever I'd attempted to create a social life for myself as if he stood next to me. *'Don't make a fool of yourself. Surely by now you've figured out people don't want to be around you. Nobody likes a loser.'* I had hoped the distance between us would diminish his power over my thoughts. I'd been wrong.

Across the road, two more men entered the club. They exchanged a few words with the bouncers and a burst of laughter reached my ears. I studied them. They looked just like me — nothing made them stand out as special or remarkable. Tight jeans, even tighter T-shirts, and loafers. Nothing about their appearance distinguished them from the people who walked past the club on their way to different venues. Nothing, apart from the fact that some of them had been holding hands and others had their arms wrapped around each other, or hands stuffed into each other's back pockets. Nothing, except that couples entering this club were either all male or all female.

That stood out like a red flag in a black-and-white movie. I couldn't imagine ever seeing that back home. The sight filled me with a longing so deep it hurt. I closed my eyes for a moment and allowed the soft June breeze to wash over me. I wanted to believe I could be one of those men one day. Nineteen years of being told I was nothing — not good enough, a disappointment as well as a disgrace — had me convinced my dream would always be that, a futile fantasy.

Time passed and I just stood there. I had to make up my mind — either bite the bullet, cross the road and enter the club or go back home. There would be no shame in going back to my house. I'd only arrived in Dublin two days ago. I didn't have to hurry or force myself. This city was home now. I could visit this club and others like it whenever I wanted, or rather, whenever I found the courage. I half turned to start the short walk home before stopping myself. *No.* If I chickened out now I might never be brave enough to take the first step. Before I could change my mind again I stepped away from the wall, crossed the street and walked up to the door.

"Sorry, mate, we'll need to see your ID."

The bouncer sounded kind enough, but his words still left me fuming inside as I pulled my wallet out of my pocket and handed my age card over. Looking like a sixteen year old when my nineteenth birthday was months behind me sucked.

"Thanks. That's grand. Enjoy your night." The bouncers stepped aside and allowed me to enter the place I'd been longing and dreading to visit in equal measure.

What had I done? Why had I not gone home? Every instinct screamed at me to turn around and walk out again. I glimpsed bright lights, dark corners and a bar along the left hand wall before I lowered my gaze to the floor. I'd seen enough to know the place was relatively empty. A few bodies moved on the dance floor in the middle of the club and some people sat at the tables surrounding it. The music was loud and the beat traveled through my body, making my eardrums vibrate. I didn't look up while I made my way to the far end of the bar where I picked the empty stool next to the wall.

The marble-like surface of the bar wasn't interesting enough for all the attention I paid it, but I couldn't bring myself to look up, never mind study my surroundings. I waited for someone to come and tell me I wasn't welcome. It had happened whenever I'd found the courage to go out in the past and I couldn't believe the same wouldn't happen here. The setting had changed, but I was still the same as I'd always been.

"What can I get ya?" The bartender appeared out of nowhere, or maybe he'd been there all along.

"Bacardi and Coke, please." I whispered the words and wasn't surprised when I had to repeat them so he could hear me over the noise. I took advantage of the bartender having forced me to look up and studied my surroundings while I waited for my drink. The place was dimly lit and divided into various areas. On the far side, couches and coffee tables created comfortable looking seating areas. Near the door, where people were now entering in a steady flow, and at the opposite end of the large space, I saw high tables without seats. The dance floor in the middle of the room sparkled under the spotlights and steadily filled up with swaying bodies.

The bartender had moved back to the center of the bar to fix my drink and talked to a man while he did so, nodding his head when the man stopped talking. Despite the fear churning through my stomach, curiosity took over. Something about the customer with dark hair caught my attention. He was little more than a silhouette but I couldn't pull my gaze away from him until he turned his head and looked straight at me. *Shit.* Muttering the soft curse, I diverted my attention back to the marble top of the bar and traced a dark line with my finger while trying to get my breathing under control. So much for staying inconspicuous while checking out the club. I fought the urge to look back up and establish whether or not the man was still looking at me. *Don't attract attention to yourself.* The voice screamed in my head and I acknowledged its wisdom.

When my drink appeared in front of me on the bar, I paid for it without looking up or acknowledging the barman. I nearly spilled the rum and Coke as I picked it up. The combination of bubbles and alcohol hit the back of my throat as I drained half the cocktail in one gulp. Tears sprang to my eyes and I swallowed hard to keep from coughing. I couldn't do this. Admitting defeat was easier than forcing myself to be braver than I'd ever be. I'd finish my drink and go home. Being alone wasn't easy but I preferred it over the fear and tension keeping me on a knife's edge right now. Maybe once I'd lived in Dublin a while longer, after I'd gotten a better feel for the place, this would be easier. After all there was no hurry. I'd no intention of ever going back home. I had a new place to live and the rest of my life to explore it.

My heart stopped jumping in my chest and my breathing slowed down as soon as I made my decision. My hand was almost steady when I reached for my glass again.

"Are you keeping this seat for anyone?"

I banged my head against the wall next to me as the barely audible voice addressed me. The shock of pain made me careless and without stopping to think, I looked up into the face of a beautiful man before immediately looking away again. Of course it was the same man I'd been staring at only a moment ago. I could feel color rising up my cheeks, as a cold sweat broke out across my brow. I numbly shook my head and returned my gaze to the half-full glass in front of me.

I felt more than saw him sit down and could feel his gaze travel over my body. A voice in my head screamed at me to forget about the drink and just leave. I couldn't do this. God only knew who he was, what he wanted. Why did he seek me out when only a few stools along the bar were occupied? I'd thought it might be safe to come here. I shouldn't feel threatened. But what if I was wrong? What if there was no safe place for me? What if

I hadn't been singled out for the reason I'd always assumed but because I sent out this subconscious message, inviting people to bully me? I had never been able to figure out why my father detested me, why people looked down on me or why others got a kick out of hurting me, but it had been the one constant in my life. I'd no reason to believe it would be different here in Dublin.

"Is this your first time here?"

His voice was still barely discernible but I couldn't detect any hostility in it. I nodded my head, unable to find my voice and grabbed my glass. Two deep swallows was all it took to finish what remained of my drink. I placed my hands on the bar, ready to push off and leave. Before I could raise myself, his hand landed on my arm.

"Don't tell me you're leaving already. I saw you come in — you've only just arrived."

For a moment, curiosity overtook fear and I turned my head to really study him. He looked even better close up than he had from a distance. Black hair fell in unruly locks around his face, his fringe nearly hitting his dark eyes. His cheekbones stood out and created an interesting pattern of light and shadow on his face. I allowed my gaze to rest on his full, smiling lips for a moment before looking away again.

"What are you drinking?" he asked when the barman walked over and stopped in front of us.

"Bacardi and Coke. But, I'm leaving." I turned away and stood up. His hand on my arm stopped me in my tracks.

"Don't. Not on my account. If you'd rather be on your own I'll go sit somewhere else."

I looked at him again, trying to figure out what he wanted from me. The words to send him on his way were on the tip of my tongue, but I swallowed them back. I'd made myself walk into this club in the hope of meeting people who'd accept me without conditions. Telling the first person to talk to me to fuck off would not help me in my search for friends.

"I'm sorry." Even while I apologized I looked around half expecting to see a group of his friends behind him, ready to pounce on me without warning, but he appeared to be as alone as I was. "I'd like another Bacardi and Coke if the offer's still open."

He rewarded me with a huge grin. "I was right, wasn't I? You haven't been here before."

"Yes." I nodded. "Is it that obvious?" My mouth curved in a weaker version of his contagious grin, despite the doubts swirling through my head.

"Only to someone paying attention." His voice sounded warm and unthreatening. "I saw you walk in and recognized the way you behaved." He smiled a bit self-consciously. "It's not that long ago since I entered this club for the first time. It can be scary, especially when you're on your own." He paused and a slight frown appeared on his face. "I'm Aidan, by the way. Can't believe I didn't introduce myself first."

"I'm Lennart." I held out my hand. After Aidan looked at it for a second he grabbed and shook it. A blush crept up my cheeks again. Trust me to go all formal and polite and make the situation awkward, again.

"You don't sound local." Aidan smiled. "A new arrival to the fair city, are you?"

I couldn't help returning his infectious smile. "Very new. I only came to Dublin two days ago."

"And you like it?"

"I think so." His question made me think. I hadn't actually considered what I thought about Dublin, too caught up in the relief I felt now I was away from the place I'd grown to hate over the nineteen years of my life. "I haven't seen a lot of it yet."

"And on your second night here you decided to explore the local talent?"

The lopsided grin on his face combined with a quick wink did nothing to decrease my anxiety levels. "I wasn't thinking about talent." The defensive note in my voice made me cringe. "Where I'm from there are no clubs like this. I didn't know what to imagine."

"That's a shame." His smile took on a different quality, one I couldn't identify although it made me feel both insecure and flattered.

The club had gotten a lot busier while we talked and people were starting to press in on us, trying to get the bartenders' attention. I tried to stay calm but couldn't stop myself from nervously glancing over my shoulder as tension settled in my muscles and my breathing became shallow.

"You wanna go and find a seat over there?" Aidan pointed at the seating area I'd noticed earlier. "It's getting a bit cramped here, and it's only going to get worse."

I nodded my consent and followed Aidan as he made his way around to the far side of the club, grateful he didn't try to cross the dance floor and the sea of moving and grinding bodies. The club was packed now and I took advantage of the fact we were moving to drink in my surroundings. I'm not sure what I'd expected before I walked in, but I couldn't have imagined what I saw in my wildest dreams. I'm not stupid. I've always known I wasn't the only one of my kind. But to see such numbers of people just like me enjoying themselves without fear of repercussions and without feeling the need to hide, boggled my mind.

Chapter Two

I barely noticed the chairs we sat down on, transfixed as I was on the crowded dance floor. Men danced with men, women with women and nobody batted an eyelid. For a moment I allowed my imagination to run amok and pictured myself in the middle of that crowd. Even in my fantasies I wasn't quite brave enough to visualize somebody dancing with me, but it would be wonderful to just let go for once, forget about all my fears and insecurities for the duration of one or two songs.

"I'm sorry?" I'd been so lost in my thoughts I'd missed Aidan's question.

"I asked if you like what you see?" He smiled. "It's probably a stupid question. I can tell you're fascinated."

I cringed and looked away from the dance floor, embarrassed at having been caught out. "I can't get my head around people being as comfortable as everybody here seems to be. I wasn't aware of other gay people back home. I mean, there must have been others, but whoever they were they kept their sexuality well hidden."

Aidan's attention was focused on me as if we weren't in the middle of a loud and busy club. Encouraged, I told him more about the life I'd left behind in Bally-Go-Backwards.

"Our town is tiny. Everybody knows everybody and their business and, I don't know, there was this unwritten law that people shouldn't stand out — attract attention to themselves. So I tried to fit in, be like the others, but people knew. For as long as I can remember they always looked down on me, shut me out..." I allowed the sentence to trail off. I didn't want to burden this man I'd only just met — somebody I hoped might turn into a friend — with all my years of trying to survive in a hostile environment. I wanted him to like, not pity, me. Some of the details I didn't share must have been obvious regardless. Something changed in his face as he listened.

"I didn't realize how lucky I was growing up here." Aidan's voice was pensive. "Not that it's all been smooth sailing..." He didn't finish his sentence either and his expression seemed to harden for a moment. He shrugged and the easy smile returned. "But it's all good now, isn't it? You don't have to go back to where you came from, do you?"

For the first time that evening the smile on my face came straight from my heart. "No, I don't ever have to go back. The town, the people who live there, my father — all of them can go to hell as far as I'm concerned. If I never see that place again it will be too soon."

"Even your parents?" Aidan asked.

"Just my father, my mother died before my second birthday. But yes, my father is the one person I really hope to never see again." I recognized the combination of sadness and surprise on his face and added. "It's a long and not particularly happy story. I won't go into it. Trust me, though, I won't be missing him and I doubt he's even noticed my absence."

My last statement almost made me laugh out loud. My father hadn't even offered me a lift to the train station when I left. He'd stood in the hall and watched me go. My father had still been furious things hadn't turned out the way he'd hoped. His parting words still rang in my ears. *'Enjoy it while it lasts, boy, because it won't. And don't even think about turning to me when it all goes wrong. Once this door closes behind you, it stays closed.'* No, he wouldn't miss me at all, although I imagined my father cursing my name every day for the foreseeable future.

"I'm sorry. I didn't mean to spoil your evening." I addressed the frown which had formed on Aidan's face. I couldn't believe it had happened again. I'd met Aidan all of an hour ago and I had already managed to alienate him. It had to be some special talent of mine. *How to alienate people and never make friends*, I should write the book.

"What? No." Aidan stared at me. "You didn't spoil anything. I just have a hard time getting my head around parents who abandon their own children."

We both stared at the dancing crowd for a moment before he continued. "Besides, you're here now. You can start a new life on your own terms. It's time to start having fun, don't you think?"

Fun? I'm not sure I'd recognize fun if it jumped up and hit me in the face. My inner critic reared its ugly head again. When I answered Aidan my voice was harder than it had been, as I attempted to drown out the internal dialogue.

"I am having fun. I didn't think I would but I really am. Thank you." I cringed inwardly. Did I have to make myself sound as needy as I just did? If Aidan noticed he was too polite to comment on it.

"You wanna dance?"

Every muscle in my body tensed at his suggestion. Imagining myself on the dance floor was one thing. To actually get up and move among the swaying crowd took far more confidence than I had.

Aidan didn't give me a chance to say no. He got out of his chair and held out his hand. When I grabbed it he pulled me up and held on to my hand as he led the way to the middle of the floor.

The acoustics in the club were phenomenal. The difference between the volume levels on the dance floor and where we'd been sitting took me by surprise. Now, in the middle of the fray, the rhythm took hold of my body. I felt the heavy bass vibrating in the floor and traveling up my legs. I should have been too self-conscious to dance but I couldn't resist the combination of beat and moving bodies. Almost against my will, my body swayed along with the rhythm. Pride filled me when a huge grin spread across Aidan's face as he watched me crawl out of my shell. His hand, still holding mine, gave me the confidence to let go of my inhibitions for a minute.

I stopped thinking as I lost myself in the music. My usual shyness disappeared, the cynical voice in my head couldn't be heard over the beat. Even Aidan letting go of my hand and throwing himself into the music couldn't put a dent in my newfound confidence. This was what I'd hoped for when I moved to Dublin, this sense of freedom, the permission to be myself, and the opportunity to stop worrying about what impression I might be making on those around me.

"You move beautifully."

Aidan's voice only barely reached my ears but his words made me glow. We circled each other as we danced. I almost froze when Aidan got very close behind me and ground his crotch into my arse.

"Relax. It's all good. Everybody here is just like you and me. Look."

I did look. Between the smoke machines and the blinding lights, it wasn't easy to see anybody in detail, which reassured me. If I couldn't see them, they couldn't see me. But what I did see showed me Aidan's grinding was as innocent as interactions on this dance floor got. A lot of couples might have been having full on sex if it weren't for the clothes they wore. Groins pressed into arses, hands explored the outlines of cocks and tonsil tennis appeared to be the taste of the day. And that was just the men. The female couples I spotted had no more inhibitions than their male counterparts. It was an exhilarating experience and my body couldn't help but respond. The stirring in my pants as blood found its way to my cock felt both delicious and uncomfortable. Part of me couldn't help but be afraid people might notice and make fun of me even while common sense told me I did not stand out in this crowd.

Songs ended and others started and our bodies moved. I'd never felt this good in my life. The sense of freedom was intoxicating. I remembered how I'd wanted to walk away from this club and Aidan. Gratitude for whatever it had been that had made me stay, filled me. My new life was turning out much better than I could have hoped.

The music changed. The beat all but disappeared as a much slower song started. I'd taken one step back toward where we'd been sitting when Aidan grabbed my shoulder and pulled me close. "Don't walk away. This is where it gets real good."

Not that I had much of a choice. With one hand holding the back of my neck and another just above my arse, I couldn't have walked away without violently dislodging myself from his hold. No matter how much the closeness scared me, I didn't want it to end and lose the opportunity to discover what it felt like to hold somebody's body close to mine.

When he pulled me closer I went. A sigh escaped me when our chests connected. With Aidan slightly taller than me, my nose ended up against his neck, just below his ear and I inhaled his aroma. Sweat combined with something earthy I couldn't name, captivated me. I closed my eyes and surrendered to the heady combination of music and Aidan. Our crotches touched and the realization my cock wasn't the only one reacting to our closeness sent a rush through me. He moved his hips and I followed his movements. Our bodies rubbing off each other brought me pleasure and frustration in equal measure.

"I told you it would be good."

Even with the music as loud as it was I could hear the heat in Aidan's voice.

"I didn't know." The words escaped my mouth before I could think about them.

"Didn't know how it would feel to dance with a man?"

I had no idea how to answer Aidan's question. I couldn't tell him I didn't know what it might be like to do anything with a man, dancing, kissing, touching. I had no experience with any of it so I just shook my head and kept quiet.

"Hey, look at me." Aidan's voice was so soft I had to strain to hear him. "Enjoy. It doesn't matter if it's a first for you. All of us had to start somewhere at some time."

I didn't know whether to be grateful or scared that he saw right through me. How could he possibly know my thoughts and feelings? We'd only just met. He didn't know me any better than I knew him and yet he seemed to have a very clear picture of who and what I was. I looked at him and saw something in his eyes that took my breath away. His heated gaze flicked from my eyes to my mouth and back again before he moved closer and pressed his lips against mine for a moment.

My body tensed and stopped moving. My heart thundered in my chest and my breathing sped up. I pulled back with enough force to break Aidan's hold and stepped away. My gaze flew around the club until I'd located the exit. I strode toward it without looking at anybody, panic driving me forward. I vaguely heard my name and ignored it. I needed to get outside, away from all these people, away from the new experiences and away from all these feelings I didn't know how to deal with.

I'm not sure I took a single breath while pushing my way toward the door. Only when I was safely on the footpath in front of the club did I allow myself to inhale a lung full of fresh air. My relief at being away from the situation that had triggered all my anxieties was short lived. As soon as my heartbeat slowed down again the full implication of what I'd just done hit me. I'd run away from a man who might have been a friend. I turned my back on somebody who'd had the patience to put up with my unsociable behavior.

That's why you're alone. You don't deserve friends. My internal tormentor didn't waste a moment, and for once I didn't try to argue with him. He was probably right.

Aidan had given me a soft kiss, nothing more. Why had I panicked? I shrugged the question off. It didn't matter. I had well and truly ruined whatever might have been with my childish behavior. I didn't turn around to look back at the club where I'd known a few happy hours, before walking away.

"Wait. Lennart. Wait."

Running footsteps approached me. For a moment I considered taking off and making sure he wouldn't catch me. Torn between not wanting to face Aidan after my shameful departure and hoping that maybe I hadn't managed to scare him off, I waited until he caught up with me. Even if he'd only chased me to tell me how big a wanker he thought I was, it wouldn't make the situation any worse. And although I knew the chances were slim, I couldn't help hoping he'd followed me because he did want to be friends, despite my foolishness.

"I'm sorry." Aidan was out of breath when he reached me and his words escaped his mouth on big gulps of air. "I should have known better. How angry are you?"

"I..." Lost for words, I stared at him. "I'm not angry. Don't say you're sorry. My childish reaction is not your fault. If anybody should apologize, it's me. And I do." I should have stopped there but the words just kept on coming. "Look, I know I'm a fool. Just walk away and forget you ever met me. I'm sorry I ruined your night."

Aidan tilted his head and examined me for a moment. "Dear Mother of God, they really did a number on you, didn't they? You didn't ruin anything and I don't want to forget I met you. I enjoyed our evening."

"So did I." I whispered the words, afraid I might spoil the moment if I talked out loud.

"You're on your way home now?" he asked.

"Yes. It's just a few streets away." I vaguely pointed in the direction I'd been walking before he caught up with me.

"Can I walk with you?" Hearing uncertainty in Aidan's voice took me by surprise. His quiet confidence had impressed me throughout the night and it bothered me my hasty reaction had stripped him of it.

"Yes. Of course. I'd like that."

We walked in almost complete silence, close together but not quite touching. Our lack of communication should have been uncomfortable but wasn't. I enjoyed his company and appreciated the opportunity to just walk together without having to search for words or worry about saying the wrong thing.

It only took ten minutes to get to my front door. Aidan let out a low whistle when he saw where I lived. "You're renting a room here, on Adelaide Road? Nice one, mate."

"No, not quite." My embarrassment was back with full force. "All of this is mine." I pointed at the three-story building in front of us in what was one of the most expensive areas in Dublin.

"You own that?" Aidan's voice held a mix of disbelief and awe.

"It's a long story but yes, I do. I inherited it off a grandfather I didn't even know I had until three months ago."

Aidan whistled again. "Man, you're set up for life."

I laughed. "I know, right? I still don't know how I got this lucky." I saw the look on Aidan's face and realized what that must have sounded like. "Listen, I'm sorry my grandfather is dead. I'm even more sorry I never got to meet him. But it's hard to mourn somebody I never knew and this house couldn't have come at a better time."

I'd been racking my brains trying to figure out how I would manage moving away from home after my exams. I'd hardly any money of my own and my father had told me he'd no intention of sponsoring my independence. When the solicitor's letter had arrived it had been an answer to all my prayers. Of course it had also been the start of a whole new set of problems with my father, but one thing or another had triggered those for as long as I could remember.

"You want to come in?" I stared at my feet while I asked the question, suddenly shy again.

"I'd love to, but not now." Aidan paused. "It's late and you've had enough excitement for one night."

I barely heard his words. Here it was, the one thing I'd known would come. Aidan would walk away and I'd never see him again.

"Lennart?" Aidan's voice broke through my thoughts. "Look at me for a moment."

I looked up from my feet, ready to encounter the pity in his eyes, only to find none. "Give me your phone."

I had no idea what he wanted but handed my phone over anyway and watched as he punched something in. "There, you've got my number now. I'm just sending myself a text so I have yours too."

I heard the muffled message received sound coming from his pocket before he handed my phone back to me.

"I want to get to know you." The way Aidan looked at me I had no doubt he meant the words. "But I'm done spooking you. So I'm going to ask you a question and your answer doesn't matter. I want to be friends regardless, okay?"

Utterly confused, I could only nod my head.

"If I kiss you, will you run again?"

If he kisses you he'll know you've never done it before. The voice was back, jumping on another opportunity to sabotage me but I ignored it.

"No. I won't run." I held my breath as Aidan closed the short distance between us. He touched my cheek and looked straight into my eyes, forcing me to look back at him. This time his lips didn't take me by surprise when they pressed against mine. The emotions the soft touch evoked in me did. I didn't panic and never thought about fleeing. Quite the opposite, I yearned for more and pressed my lips against his in a quiet demand.

Feeling his lips curve under mine before parting filled me with wonder. I gasped when his tongue stroked my mouth and Aidan took full advantage of my reaction. I remembered reading somewhere that you never forget your first kiss and in that moment I knew it to be true. What on earth had I been worried about? I might be clueless but my mouth and tongue knew exactly what to do as the kiss got deeper. He explored my mouth and I explored his, lost in feelings so heady I felt faint.

He pulled me closer until not even air flowed between our bodies. When our crotches made contact, desire ran down my spine in shivers I couldn't conceal. I moved my pelvis, searching for more…more contact, more new sensations and more heat.

When he pulled back, both of us were breathing hard. His face lit up with a smile so radiant I couldn't help but mirror it. Aidan rested his forehead against mine. "A much better way to end our evening. I'll call you in the morning."

Fear tried to rear its ugly head again. My internal voice screamed at me that I would never see nor hear from him again. It took more courage than I thought I had but I pressed my lips against his one last time before turning around and walking to my front door. "I'd like that. Maybe we could meet, do something?" I held my breath, afraid to turn and look at him.

"Yes, I like the sound of that. See you tomorrow."

I opened the door and turned to look at the man who'd changed my world in one evening. He stood underneath the streetlight and smiled. I made sure to capture the image in my memory before closing the door. Just in case.

Chapter Three

The buzzing sound pulling me from a deep sleep was unfamiliar. I opened my eyes and for a few seconds I had no idea where I was. I looked around my bedroom and a smile settled on my face as recognition dawned. Most of the furniture in the big room was hidden in dark shadows but enough sunlight shone through the heavy, floor-length curtains to make my surroundings look magical.

When my gaze landed on the bedside table and my flashing mobile phone I knew what my wake-up call had been. No wonder it had taken me a moment to figure out what I'd heard. This would be only the second text message I'd ever received on this phone. Nobody had my number. Well, nobody except for…Aidan.

I nearly fell out of bed in my haste to find out what he might have sent me.

Morning. Hope I didn't wake u. It's a great day. Wanna hang out?

I grinned as I stared at his short message. He'd really meant it. Despite my best efforts to make a fool of myself he still wanted to get to know me. All too familiar insecurities tried to push themselves to the forefront of my mind but I forced them back and concentrated on the words on the small screen.

For around half a second I thought about playing it cool, then I allowed my fingers to do the talking.

Would love to meet up. Tell me when and where and I'll be there.

I hit send before I could worry about whether or not that sounded too eager or needy. His reply arrived moments after I'd sent mine.

Great. Meet you in Stephen's Green at the statue of the Three Fates in about an hour?

I knew where the park was although I'd no idea about the statue. Still, Stephen's Green wasn't so big I wouldn't be able to find it.

Sure. C U there. Thanks

I nearly deleted the last word. Even after I'd sent the reply I wondered if 'thanks' hadn't been too much. By then it was too late to take it back and I had meant it. I also didn't have time for these reflections. I'd a date with a man who'd more than piqued my interest in less than an hour. Unless I wanted to be late I'd better get out of bed and start moving.

While hot water streamed down my body in the shower I took my time to reflect on the previous night. By the time I'd closed the front door behind me I'd been so exhausted it had taken all my strength just to drag my body up the stairs to the bedroom. I'd fallen asleep the moment my head hit my pillow and only now realized how peaceful the night had been. I hadn't woken up several times to agonize over my behavior in the club or been plagued by nightmares. It had to be a first for me.

Memories of my evening with Aidan rushed through my mind. I forced myself to ignore my idiotic display of insecurity and concentrated on all that'd been wonderful about it. Meeting Aidan, dancing, losing myself in the music and that kiss, his body against mine, our cocks rubbing together through our pants. I closed my eyes and relived the moment, barely aware of my soapy hand stroking my hard-on.

Kissing had been so much better than I'd ever imagined. For years I'd pitied myself. The only one my age never to have kissed or have been kissed. Right now I could only be happy it had taken so long. What I'd experienced last night had to be the perfect first kiss. There'd been nothing clumsy or awkward about it, at least, I didn't think so. I couldn't be sure of course but thought I would have known if it hadn't been right.

Heat curled in my belly and my balls tightened as I stroked myself faster. I imagined dark eyes staring at me from below a black fringe as I came in a short and sharp orgasm.

It took me forever to decide what to wear. I'd never been vain or worried about my clothes and appearance but that day I wanted to get it right. Within ten minutes my bed covers were invisible underneath a layer of discarded tops, trousers and shorts. I looked out the window at the cloudless sky and settled on cut-off jeans and a white T-shirt with a bright rainbow across the front. I'd bought the shirt on my first afternoon in

Dublin, unsure if I'd ever be brave enough to wear it. Now that I'd allowed myself to step out of my comfort zone and was about to push my boundaries even further, the shirt didn't seem quite so daring any more.

When I stared at my reflection in the mirror I had to fight the impulse to change into something else. No matter what I wore I would always be the pale kid with red hair and freckles. I would stand out like a sore thumb next to Aidan with his black hair and dark eyes. I hadn't been able to see it last night but I'd no doubt he'd have a healthy tan, something I would never achieve with my skin, bright red was both the best and the worst I could hope for.

I sighed and glanced at my phone only to be shocked into action. I had barely fifteen minutes left before I was supposed to meet Aidan and I needed at least ten of them to get to the park. Which left me five short minutes to find that statue he'd mentioned. Without a backward glance I rushed down the stairs and out the door.

The park was busy, even this early on a Saturday morning. Given the unpredictability of Irish summers it didn't surprise me but it made walking fast harder than I wanted it to be. With about a minute to spare I spotted the statue of The Three Fates and Aidan standing beside it. I stopped walking so abruptly somebody bumped into my back and cursed at me before pushing around me.

I couldn't make myself take the last few steps. The curses the passerby had thrown at me echoed in my head and brought back unwanted memories. *'What are you doing here? You didn't really think we wanted to hang out with you, did you? Fuck off, you wanker.'* And the one that always hurt most because it had come from my father at a time when I'd still hoped he might love me.

'*Of course he doesn't want to play with you, you're such an awkward child.*' I'd been nine when my father said those words and it had been the last time I'd invited someone over for a playdate.

As I stared at the man who was even more beautiful than I remembered, doubt assailed me. I couldn't imagine him being interested in me.

I couldn't do it. If I walked away now the memory of last night would remain unsullied. I took a step backwards and was about to turn around and walk back the way I'd come when Aidan spotted me. A huge grin spread across his face as he closed the distance between us.

"Hi. I was about to send you a message. I thought maybe you didn't know where the statue was."

I couldn't hear any trace of meanness or sarcasm in his voice no matter how hard I listened for it.

"I didn't." I forced myself not to look at my feet. "But the park isn't that big and there's a handy sign with all the landmarks near the entrance."

"Right. I forgot about that." He smiled and bent toward me before placing a soft kiss on my lips. "I'm glad you could make it. What would you like to do?"

The kiss startled and reassured me. I couldn't stop myself from glancing around, convinced somebody would pounce on us for that minor display of affection. If anybody had noticed they didn't seem to mind as far as I could tell. "Would you show me around? I don't know where anything is in this city." I hesitated. "I need to have breakfast first, if you don't mind. I'm starving and didn't have time to eat before I left the house."

"Perfect." His infectious grin was back. "I didn't eat either. Couldn't wait to get out when I saw the nice weather. Come, I know the perfect place."

We had breakfast in a small coffee shop not too far away from the park. I don't know whether it was the food or the company but the Full Irish had never tasted as wonderful before. We gorged ourselves on bacon, sausages, eggs, beans, black and white pudding and slice after slice of warm, buttered toast. The tea was strong and sweet and being with Aidan was easy. He chatted away and if he noticed how hard small talk was for me, he didn't show it. We walked through town for hours. Aidan showed me great places to shop, cozy pubs, wonderful short cuts and hidden squares and alleys I would never have found on my own. The sun beat down on us and it wasn't long before I realized I'd need sunscreen unless I wanted to end the day in pain.

Aidan burst out laughing when I finished applying a liberal amount of factor fifty to my pale skin. "You're supposed to rub it in, you know."

"What?" I stared at my arms and legs and saw no sign of residue.

"Bend your neck." Aidan stepped behind me and massaged the bits I'd missed into my already overheated skin with soft strokes. His touch was light and I had no doubt he took much longer than necessary. Just for a moment I allowed my eyes to close. His fingers on my flesh awakened new and intoxicating feelings in me. My over-active brain couldn't stop itself from imagining his touch on other parts of my body. And one of those parts stirred in my pants at the thought.

"I love your skin." He whispered the words into my ear. "It's so beautiful and white, so soft to my touch."

I sighed, too content to doubt his words even if I'd never thought of my paleness as anything but ugly and inconvenient. I missed his touch the moment he stopped caressing my neck.

"Come, I'll show you where I work. It's only around the corner." Aidan took the lead again and led me to a big shop on one of the canals. I stared at the name for a moment.

"The Hidden Universe, what sort of a shop is that?" The window I faced displayed posters of Doctor Who, Harry Potter and Star Trek.

"Oh" — just for a moment Aidan looked self-conscious — "it's the ultimate geek's paradise. Let's go in and you can tell me what you think."

As soon as we entered the shop, Aidan got called over by a big man behind a cash register and I let him walk away as I lost myself in what looked like a dream come true. For years I'd dreamt about filling my room with the kind of knickknacks they sold here. Miniature TARDISes, magic wands, action figures from numerous movies and books, so many books. I rummaged through the graphic novels, losing track of time as I tried to decide how many I could bring home with me without embarrassing myself.

"There you are." Aidan's voice brought me back to earth. "You like this place then?"

"Oh my God, this shop is perfect. I can't believe you work here. I'd put in the hours for free." I couldn't hide my enthusiasm. "I could lose myself here for days without noticing time passing." I was surprised to see relief appear on Aidan's face as I talked. "Who wouldn't love working in a place like this?"

"You'd be surprised." For a moment Aidan didn't resemble the easy-going man I thought I knew, then his expression shifted back and I looked at the relaxed version of him again.

"Let's go. Much as I love this place, I spend enough time here without wanting to stay for hours when I'm not working." Aidan walked toward the door. With a reluctant glance at the books I had to leave behind I followed him. "If you like it here you can always come to visit me when I'm working. We could have lunch together or something."

My heart lifted at his words. He still wanted to see more of me. He was about to set a record. I pushed the thought out of my head.

"Yeah. I'd like that." I smiled as I made the understatement of the year. Dublin was turning out to be so much better than I'd dared to hope in even my wildest fantasies.

Back outside, we walked along the canal for a short while before Aidan led the way through a small archway into an even smaller alley. The place was packed. Music blasted out of shops on both sides of us and we had to push our way through groups of tourists as they tried to fight their way to the next place of interest.

The crowds pressed too close and the noise made thinking impossible. Happiness drained from me as anxiety built, leaving me tense and on high alert. I fixed my gaze on Aidan's back as he walked a few steps ahead of me. *I won't panic. I won't panic. I won't panic.* I kept on repeating the words in my head as we walked toward the end of the alley and sighed in relief when we arrived on a wider street.

"Are you okay?"

"I'm okay. Now. I'm sorry. I'm not good in crowds." I looked up and down the street and my heart sank because it appeared almost as busy as the alley we'd left. "Where are we?"

"Temple Bar." Aidan smiled. "Dublin's infamous tourist and nightlife center. I thought we could find a restaurant here and have dinner."

I battled with myself and lost. "I'm sorry. Could I take a rain check on that? I need to get away from the crowds. It's…" I couldn't go on, even talking about how the moving masses made me feel increased my panic levels.

Aidan stepped closer to me, grabbed my hand and squeezed it. "It's okay. We don't need to do anything you don't want to do. If you want to go home and spend some time alone, that's fine."

The disappointment I saw on his face made me both happy and disgusted with myself. "It's not that I want to be alone." I took a deep breath and decided to be brave for a change. "I enjoy spending time with you. I just need to get away from all these people. If you want…" I hesitated, gathered up all my courage and ignored the fear of rejection. "We could go to my place and order dinner in?"

If I'd been even slightly less self-conscious I would have kissed him there and then when he agreed to my suggestion.

Chapter Four

"All of this is yours?" Aidan's amazement mirrored the feelings I'd had when I'd first walked into my house.

"Tell me about it. I still can't get over it. I would have settled for a room the size of a closet. Want me to show you around before we order food?"

"Sure."

Aidan sounded excited at the prospect. I closed the front door behind us and walked toward the stairs. "Let's start upstairs. We'll be hanging down here later on anyway." As we ascended the stairs I grew evermore shy. I had nothing to be ashamed of, but I knew nineteen year-old kids didn't usually own their own houses and I couldn't help worrying what it might look like to Aidan.

"Where do you live?" I glanced over my shoulder at Aidan just in time to see a frown cross his face.

"I share a house in Phibsboro, over on the Northside with three other lads." His tone made it clear he didn't want to say anything else about the topic. I ignored my curiosity and all the questions I wanted to ask and opened a door.

"There's three bedrooms here. This one I plan to use as a study."

Aidan smiled. "A study. Cool. Are you starting college in September?"

"No." I wished I'd kept my plans for this room to myself. I didn't know him well enough to share my dreams with him. I couldn't stand the idea he might laugh at me.

"What do you need a study for then?" Aidan stood in the center of the room and stared at the walls lined with overflowing bookshelves.

I looked away. "I do a bit of…" I mumbled the last word so softly even I couldn't hear it.

"You do a bit of what? Tell me. How bad can it be?"

I had his full attention now. "Writing." I spit the word at him and prepared myself for the inevitable burst of laughter.

"You write?" Rather than scorn I heard awe in his voice. "That's so cool. Are you any good? What do you write? Can I read it?" His questions nearly overwhelmed me and caused heat to travel from my neck onto my cheeks.

"I don't know if I'm any good." I hesitated. "I've been writing for years but thought it would never be more than a hobby. With the inheritance, I can afford to take some time and see if it could lead to anything." I wasn't rich or anything, but besides the house I'd also inherited enough money to keep me going for a few years if I didn't start spending like a madman.

My hope that he might have forgotten his other questions disappeared as soon as Aidan opened his mouth again. "What sort of stories do you write?"

His question made the heat, which had just started to recede from my cheeks, turn into a full on blush. "I've started this fantasy for young adults recently." Words fell from my mouth as my shyness receded. "I quite like where it's going and I've lots of ideas for the rest of that story. The other one…" I allowed the sentence to trail off while I wondered why I'd even mentioned that second story.

"What about the other one?"

"It's…" I lowered my gaze and studied the floor and my feet as I tried to decide whether I was brave enough to take the risk. I peeked at Aidan's face. Curiosity shone in his eyes and pushed me forward.

"That one's a romance." I didn't say the words *so what*, but I'm sure Aidan heard them regardless.

"I like romances." Aidan said it as if it was the most normal thing in the world for a man to admit to. "Well, I like gay romances."

He didn't need to ask the question. The tilt of his head and his raised eyebrow made it perfectly clear what he wanted to know.

"Yes. It's an all-male romance. I haven't gotten very far in that story yet though."

Aidan looked at me with a thoughtful expression on his face. "Is that because you've only started the story or…?" He left the rest of his question hanging.

The lie almost left my mouth. It would have been so easy to tell him I'd only started the story a few weeks ago. Instead I said nothing in the hope that ignoring the question would make it go away. I couldn't bring myself to admit that unless and until I got some personal experience with a man I couldn't see myself making any progress with that book.

A lazy smile spread across his face. "I think I know what you need. You're looking for inspiration, aren't you?"

Again I had to fight the temptation to lie to him. Telling him the truth didn't feel like an option either, so I went with a half-truth. "I'll never say no to new ideas if you have any." I returned his smile and hoped against hope my blush didn't give the game away.

"Show me the rest of your house first and feed me. Then I'll see what I can do about helping you conquer your writer's block."

His smile turned into a full on and mildly dirty grin, which made my stomach all fluttery and my cock pay attention.

The guest bedroom wasn't much to look at, an unmade double bed and a wall worth of empty closets. I hesitated before I opened the door to my bedroom. I couldn't remember how I'd left it when I'd rushed out in the morning and worried bringing him there might be too forward.

Before I could make up my mind, Aidan turned the handle and walked in. I flinched when I spotted the unmade bed and the discarded clothes scattered across it. Aidan stared at the mess before turning to me with a smile on his face.

"I'm glad you picked that shirt." His touch flittered across my chest. "I'm rather fond of rainbows."

Suddenly shy again, I turned and walked to the bed. I picked up the discarded clothes and dumped them into my wardrobe without regard for where they landed before glancing around the room. It didn't reflect my personality any more than the rest of the house did. Slightly bigger than the guest room, mine only distinguished itself in that the bed had covers and that I'd brought some books in here for late night reading.

"There's not a lot to see." I should have thought about the bareness of the house before I offered to show him around. "I haven't been here long enough yet to decide what to do with all this space. There's so much of it, and I've never had to decorate anything."

"That's okay. I love seeing this house as it is. Man, the things you could do. And to think it's all yours. If you wanted to paint all the walls purple nobody would be able to stop you."

I burst out laughing as I looked at the walls and imagined them purple, and it wasn't long before he joined me.

"Let's go down stairs and order dinner. I'm starving." Still out of breath, I walked into the hall.

"What's up there?" Aidan pointed at the third floor.

"The attic. It's been partitioned into two more rooms you can't really use for anything besides storage. The windows are tiny and the roof is too low. Right now they're full of boxes. The solicitor said my granddad had all his personal stuff stored up there. I guess I'll have to go through it someday." I shrugged. "Like I said, I've only been here for three days. That stuff can wait."

"Aren't you curious?" Aidan stopped walking when he reached the ground floor and turned to look up at me. "Didn't you say you never knew this grandparent existed until he died?"

"Yes, I did."

"Don't you want to find out more then? I'll help you go through those boxes if you want." He looked almost excited about the prospect.

"Thanks, I'd love that. When I get around to it." Of course, the big question was whether or not I'd ever reach the point where my curiosity outweighed my fear. One look at Aidan's face told me he didn't understand my lack of enthusiasm. "Look. Yes, I am curious. I want to know who he was. But when I start digging I'll also find out why I never met him. Why my father hated him and pretended he'd died. I'm not sure I want to find the answers to those questions."

I didn't tell him I wouldn't be able to cope if my grandfather turned out to have been mean, selfish or even a criminal. Having a bastard for a father was bad enough. If it ran in the family, I didn't want to know about it.

"Anyway, what are we eating?" I grabbed some menus I'd found on the floor behind the front door when I moved in, from a drawer in the hall cabinet and handed them to Aidan. "I'm fine with anything."

While Aidan called in our order for pizza, I grabbed two beers from the almost empty fridge.

With drinks in our hands, we collapsed on the couch. For the first time since I'd arrived in Dublin I felt at home. Up until now this house had been too big for me. Especially this open plan, L-shaped living-dining-kitchen area. It surprised me how much difference the addition of one other person made. I glanced at Aidan. How had he ended up in my house, on my couch? The thought that he might be too good to be true tried to rear its ugly head, before I forced it away again. Aidan was here because he wanted to be with me. Nobody had forced him so I had to accept he might be the exception to the rule which said nobody ever stuck with me.

We chatted while we waited for our pizzas to arrive. The ease with which the conversation flowed amazed me. Aidan talked, I answered, we laughed and I relaxed. It didn't feel we'd waited long when the bell chimed. I answered the door and paid for the pizzas while Aidan got us another beer from the fridge. The next twenty minutes were spent more or less in silence as we demolished our food.

Two more beers later we were slumped on the couch. The warm sunshine we'd been out in all day combined with a full stomach and a few drinks had made both of us drowsy. I looked at Aidan and it suddenly occurred to me how little I knew about him. Out of character for me, I allowed curiosity to win out over caution.

"Are you a real Dub?"

"Yeah, born and bred. In the suburbs, though, not here."

"But you don't live at home anymore?"

"No." Aidan studied me for a moment before continuing. "I'm twenty-three and should be doing my own thing. And my parents have it hard enough without me being there."

He sounded sad and guilt about the questions I'd asked welled up in me. Before I could apologize he continued talking.

"You see, my da lost his job." His voice mesmerized me as I listened to him tell me how his parents could barely keep things together with three kids still at home and neither of them working. "If I lived at home I would pay rent, of course. But the house is small for the five people who live there now."

I felt guilty again when he told me he gave his parents money every month anyway. I had this big, expensive house all to myself for free and Aidan basically paid two rents every month on what couldn't be great wages. An idea sprang to life in my mind but I discarded it before it could take root. I knew it was much too soon to make the offer.

"And there have been incidents in the past, when I still lived with them." The tone of Aidan's voice as much as his choice of words pulled my out of my slump and made me pay real attention.

"What sort of incidents?" I had a feeling I knew the answer but couldn't stop myself from asking the question.

He looked and I knew the depth of our emerging friendship would be decided here and now. He would either trust me or he wouldn't, and I fully expected him to stop talking.

"I came out shortly after my eighteenth birthday. My family was and still is fine with it." A smile brightened his face. "They've been great about it from the start." The smile faded. "Some people in the neighborhood felt differently and decided to make their displeasure known. I moved out as soon as I'd finished the Leaving Cert exams. It wouldn't have been fair on my family if I'd stayed. The abuse and vandalism stopped as soon as I disappeared from the scene."

I listened to Aidan with my heart in my throat. I knew the sort of abuse he talked about. I'd experienced the vandalism and still had the occasional nightmare in which bullies tried to corner me. Those experiences had turned me into a coward. I looked at Aidan with new respect. He hadn't crawled into a shell, he didn't hide from the world and he had no problems in crowds or hang-ups about being true to himself. I, on the other hand…

"Hey, what's with the frown?"

Aidan's question interrupted my thoughts. I turned to face Aidan and made a conscious effort to relax my expression.

"Nothing. It's the bullying you mentioned. It brought back some memories."

"You too?" Aidan asked.

"Don't tell me that surprises you." I forced a smile onto my face. "I don't think I was born a coward, or as awkward as I am."

"Why do you call yourself a coward, or awkward?"

I bristled. Despite Aidan's surprise looking genuine, I felt ridiculed. "Excuse me. You've been spending time with me, haven't you?" Aggravation made me restless and I got up and paced the room. "You must have noticed how nervous I was last night. You saw me run away from the club. You were there when I nearly had a panic attack in Temple Bar. You've met the coward and seen the awkward. Don't pretend you didn't."

I'd been so busy ranting and stalking up and down the room I didn't notice Aidan had gotten up as well until he stood in front of me, forcing me to stop walking.

"Why are you beating yourself up over that? Do you think I'd be here if I minded?"

"I don't know." I hated the petulant note I couldn't keep out of my voice. "For all I know you're just waiting for the best opportunity to hit out at me. You wouldn't be the first."

The expression on Aidan's face stopped my flow. He looked hurt, as if I'd punched him in the face.

"Do you really think I would do that? Is that who you think I am?"

"I don't know. No! It's not what I think." Whatever anger I'd felt before disappeared. "I don't know what to think. You're too good to be true." Some of the pain had disappeared off Aidan's face, leaving him more confused than hurt looking. I sighed, "I'm sorry, it's just…"

"Just what, Lennart? I think I deserve to know why you felt the need to lash out at me."

"I'm used to people giving up on me and walking away." I didn't want to have this conversation, but I owed him some sort of explanation. "When you took my number last night, I didn't expect you to actually get in touch with me. I wouldn't have been surprised if you hadn't been in the park today. People don't like me once they get to know me. Why would I expect you to be different?"

"Because" — the last trace of anger had left his voice — "I'm not people. I don't pretend. I either like you or I don't. And trust me, if I didn't like you, I wouldn't be here."

I felt as if I'd already lost him. And for the first time ever I would have no doubt it had been my own fault. Sure I'd already ruined whatever might have been, I went for broke. "But, why are you here?"

A small smile played around his mouth, confusing me even more. "Because I like you. Because I think you're cute. And because I've been dying to do this all day."

Whatever I'd expected it hadn't been his lips on mine. He hadn't walked away after my outburst. He'd called me cute. He kissed me as if he'd never found anything tastier than my mouth. Everything his words hadn't been able to convince me of became believable while we kissed. I surrendered and hoped he could taste my apology off my lips, that my tongue tangling with his, would tell him how much I wanted to be there, with him.

Aidan pulled me closer until our bodies touched in all the important places. The bulge in his shorts against mine made me dizzy and brave. I pulled his shirt out of his trousers and explored his skin with my hands. The sensation of naked skin under my fingers was both familiar and a revelation and filled me with a sense of wonder. His chest was more hairy than mine and I loved running my fingers through the short curls. When my thumb brushed his nipple, he inhaled sharply, so I did it again. Aidan allowed me my explorations. He deepened our kiss as my hands got more adventurous.

"I want to see you." I felt the blush erupt on my cheeks as soon as the words left my mouth.

Aidan brushed his lips over my heated cheeks. "You're so cute when you blush."

His words only heightened my awkwardness. I felt lost when he pulled back but only until he pulled his shirt over his head.

I couldn't help myself and stared. Aidan looked nothing like me. My skinny body had hardly any definition at all. Aidan, on the other hand, had broad shoulders, well defined upper arms and while not quite a six-pack, a very well cut stomach. The hair on his chest was black, just like the little trail of hair disappearing into his shorts.

Aidan laughed when I licked my lips. "Like what you see?"

I nodded and reached for the button on his shorts, half expecting him to stop me.

"Whatever clothes you strip off me, I will take off you too." Aidan's voice mirrored the heat flowing through my veins.

His statement confused me for a moment, until I realized he'd given me an out. He'd put me in control of what would happen next. The idea both reassured and scared me. I had no experience with men, or women for that matter. I'd no idea how this worked, what should happen next, how far we should go. I couldn't have stopped though. I needed to see more of him. I yearned to discover what it felt like to have a naked body pressed against mine. I didn't think about all the things those bodies might do once naked.

I pushed the button through the hole and lowered the zip. After I'd grabbed the band of his shorts, I looked into his eyes, searching for permission to go on. His normally deep brown eyes had darkened to almost black.

"Are you sure?" Aidan whispered the question.

In reply I pushed his shorts down, unaware I'd also gotten hold of his boxers until his cock jumped free, hard and pointing at his belly. I stopped moving. His beauty took my breath away.

Aidan shuffled backwards when I reached for him. I wanted my hand on his cock and to discover if another cock would feel like mine. I wondered if he'd enjoy the same moves that drove me crazy when I jacked off.

"No. No touching until you're naked too." The gravelly note in his voice betrayed Aidan's arousal while his eyes sparkled with a playfulness I hadn't seen before. "I want to see you too."

I kept my gaze fixed on his body as I stripped as fast as I could while Aidan stepped out of his shorts and shoes. I started shivering as soon as I'd revealed all of me. A blush crept up my neck and cheeks again. I felt so utterly inadequate. The only part of me not looking insignificant next to Aidan's version was my cock. I expected to see disappointment on his face when I looked up at him. Instead, I found lust and admiration.

He explored my chest with his hand. I had to strain to hear his words. "So soft." I closed my eyes and followed the progress of his hand across my chest by touch alone. It had never occurred to me to play with my nipples. I would never make that mistake again. Pin pricks of pleasure shot through my body as Aidan rubbed them with his thumbs and pinched them. My cock jerked against my belly and I groaned.

He pulled me in and slammed his mouth against mine. No careful explorations this time, no playful wrestling of tongues. This was an attack. He claimed me and I surrendered.

"Are you sure you want to do this here?" He growled the words into my ear.

"No. Not here." Before I could change my mind I turned around and walked to the door, pulling Aidan with me.

Chapter Five

We didn't talk as we walked up the stairs or while we crossed the landing. I gestured for Aidan to walk into my room first, followed him in, turned, closed the door and froze. Panic settled deep in my stomach. *What the fuck am I doing?* The question screamed through my mind.

"Hey, what's wrong?"

His breath caressed my shoulder. He stood just behind me. I imagined I felt his body heat on my skin.

"We don't have to do this."

Yes we do. I needed to follow this through so badly it hurt. I had to find my way back to the heat-driven confidence I'd felt before we'd climbed the stairs.

Aidan's embrace restored some of my inner peace. His arms around my waist made me feel safe and his naked body, softly pressing into mine, underscored how badly I wanted this closeness and yet I still couldn't bring myself to speak or turn around.

I grabbed one of his hands and pulled it lower until it touched my straining cock. My body might be able to tell him what I couldn't bring myself to put into words.

"Okay." He chuckled behind me. "So it's not that you want to stop."

"No, please don't stop." His gentle strokes sent waves of pleasure through my body.

"I won't, unless you ask me to. Tell me what's wrong though."

My cheeks heated up as I tried to formulate an intelligent answer before blurting out the truth. "I don't know what to do."

"Look at me." He released my cock and turned me around before resting his forehead against mine. "You don't have to do anything. You can't really get this wrong. If it feels good, it is good."

His lips caressed mine. When his tongue traced the outline of my mouth, my fears evaporated and I pushed in closer, looking for the intimacy I'd never experienced before and craved like life-sustaining sustenance. His chest hairs tickled my bare body. When our cocks made contact heat flashed through me. The last of my fear evaporated as curiosity grew stronger.

I stroked across his cock with one of my fingers, and felt the jerking motions of his member against mine.

"Yes, touch me." His low voice betrayed his lust and further ignited mine. I grew braver and circled his cock with my hand. I knew what felt good to me, and knew of only one way to find out if he'd also enjoy it. I stroked, twisting my hand occasionally and rejoiced in the groans escaping his lips. My confidence and my movements became bolder as I took my cues from the sounds he made.

"Stop."

As soon as I heard the word I jerked my hand back, afraid I'd managed to hurt him.

"I don't want it to be over yet. We've only just started." He smiled and took my hand to lead me to the bed. "Lie down. I want to look at you."

I stretched out on the bed, and turned my head away from Aidan.

"God, man, I love your body." Aidan's words shocked me into turning my head to look at him. Far from disappointment or even disgust I saw heat on his face. "I want to taste all of you, run my tongue along your stomach. I want to bite your nipples and lick your balls."

His words proved as powerful as his touch. I couldn't keep still under his heated gaze and shifted around on top of the covers. I stilled again when he got on the bed and sat down on my thighs, his cock cruelly only inches away from mine. He bent forward and plundered my mouth with his. The heat in his kiss nearly overwhelmed me. His touch appeared to be everywhere on my skin at once, stroking my neck, tickling my sides, teasing my nipples and driving me crazy. I tried to push up, get closer to him. His weight on my legs and his hands on my upper body held me in place as if he'd tied me up.

I missed his tongue the second he stopped kissing me. When his lips found one of my nipples and caressed it, gooseflesh erupted on my skin. The scrape of his teeth over the ever more sensitive area made me buck my hips despite his weight holding me down. "You're so hot." Aidan's words poured more fuel on the fire raging unrestricted through my body. A small voice in the back on my head insisted Aidan was wrong but for once my inner tormentor didn't stand a chance. No amount of insecurity could make me doubt the heat in his kiss, the attraction in his eyes or the message his leaking cock gave me. Right or wrong, I did turn him on. It was enough. It was more than I'd ever dared hope for. My wildest dreams, my most exotic fantasies, hadn't been able to conjure up images and feelings like these.

"Turn on your side." He murmured the words against my lips as he moved his weight off my legs. We faced each other and he pulled my groin closer to his until our cocks touched. "Give me your hand." My free will had disappeared. He asked or demanded and I did, without doubt or second thought.

He entwined our fingers and brought our joined hands to our cocks. "Move with me." We stroked our cocks, my hand rubbing his and his hand touching mine. The friction where our cocks rubbed off each other took my breath away. I wanted to look at him, print the image of his lust-filled face in my mind forever but the feelings were too strong. Pleasure ran through my body and I closed my eyes to feel more. The intensity didn't compare to anything I'd experienced on my own. Alone I would rush the climax. Here, with Aidan I wanted to draw it out, make it last forever. I knew any orgasms I'd given myself in the past would pale into insignificance set against what would follow soon. I yearned to reach that climax as much as I didn't want to lose this wonderful sense of togetherness.

Noises filled the room. It took me a minute before I realized at least a few of them came from my mouth. "I'm so close. Aidan, please." I'd no idea what I begged him for.

"Yes. Let it go. You feel so good." Pressure built in my stomach and balls. It wouldn't take much more. Knowing our joint hand job affected Aidan as much as it did me was almost enough to undo me as soon as he said the words.

My mind blanked when I came. The sensation traveled through my body, clenching and tensing my muscles. The sound coming from my mouth could only be described as a scream as my balls drew up and hot cum erupted against our bellies. Aidan didn't let go of my hand and a few strokes later he joined me, his release mixing with mine on our bodies.

Our cocks slowly shrank beneath our hands until they fell free and we lay there, our fingers still entwined. Drowsiness descended on me and my mind began to drift before Aidan's voice pulled me back to the present. "Are you okay?"

I blinked my eyes open and stared at him. "God yes. I'm so much better than okay I don't know where to begin."

"Did your first time live up to your expectations?" Aidan's gaze was fixed on my eyes and didn't allow me to look away.

My insecurities returned with a vengeance. "Did I do it wrong?"

The lazy smile stretching across his face brought some reassurance. "Wrong? Man, I don't remember it ever feeling this right." He stroked my cheek and turned serious. "I need you to stop doubting you, or me. There is no shame in this being your first time. It happens when it happens and provided you're lucky enough to be with a considerate partner, the first time should be magical." A cloud seemed to pass over his expression, robbing his face of all the pleasure I'd seen there only a second ago, before he relaxed again.

"I didn't disappoint then?"

"Why would you think that?" Aidan sounded utterly confused.

"How would I know?" I looked at Aidan and saw he still didn't get it. "I've got nothing to compare it to. I know I've never felt anything like that before. But I can't tell whether it was good for you or not. I don't know if you wanted more or…" I let the words trail off.

"Hey" — he smiled at me — "I wanted to be with you, and I was. You have this awesome body I can't get enough of and the most wonderful cock I've got lots of plans for. Yes, tonight was good for me. No, I didn't expect or hope for anything else or anything more than we did. I…" For the first time since we'd met, Aidan appeared to be lost for words.

"What?" The wistful expression on his face made me curious.

"I'm glad I'm your first. I want to introduce you to all the pleasure your body can give and receive."

Even through his tan I could see the blush forming on his cheeks. I moved in and kissed him, lost for words and filled with gratitude for this man I'd met less than twenty-four hours ago. He'd no idea, but he'd transformed my life. In my head, next to the voice always criticizing me, another one had taken up residence. The new, barely discernible voice whispered in the background, suggesting I might be good enough after all.

"Are you staying?"

"Would you like me to?" Aidan's question took me by surprise. I wanted nothing more than to fall asleep with him close, maybe even with his arm around me.

"Yes. I'd like it if you stayed."

Aidan stretched out and smiled. "I think it's going to be my pleasure."

Chapter Six

It had been early when we'd moved to the bedroom and although we'd dozed off after our talk, the evening was far from over. I'm not sure how long we slept. When I woke up with Aidan curled up against me and his arm slung over my chest, I felt happier than I'd ever been. I forced my body to stay still. I wanted to revel in the closeness for as long as possible, memorize the feelings it gave me. His cock pressed against my arse and I lost myself in fantasies both enticing and terrifying. I wanted to know what it would be like to have a cock inside me, but not right now. The stiffness of his cock had an immediate effect on mine and I touched my stiff member, surprised and delighted to discover it had recovered already.

"Are you touching yourself?" Aidan sounded sleepy and hoarse. "We can't have that, you know. Either you show me what you're doing or you let me do the touching."

I froze, afraid I'd made a mistake. Then the humorous undercurrent in Aidan's words and voice got through to me and I relaxed. "And do you have a preference?"

I'd no idea where this playful version of me came from or where he'd been hiding all my life, but I liked him.

"Oh, I love watching. And I like touching. Can I watch first?"

I hesitated for a moment. Was I really brave enough to let him watch me while I played with myself?

"You're thinking again." His soft words broke through my thoughts. "Just do it. I know you're hard and hot. I know you want to grab your cock and stroke it, pull it until the need builds and all you can think about is the release, just a few strokes away. Go on. There's nothing you can show me I haven't done myself. Seeing you would be so good."

His words hypnotized me. As I stroked myself my doubts evaporated to be replaced by lust and need. I didn't stop giving myself pleasure as he turned me onto my back. His gaze was fixed on my crotch, his pupils darker than I'd seen them yet. Far from embarrassed I felt powerful. My body, the same body I'd hated for years, made him hot enough to lick his lips.

As soon as I thought about his lips, my imagination conjured up the picture of his mouth on my cock. As if he'd read my mind, Aidan shifted on the bed until his head rested on my thigh, his mouth just inches away from my cock. I stopped moving my hand and held my breath as I watched him.

"Look at you." Need sounded in his voice. "You're leaking. I wonder what you taste like."

Before I could think about his words his tongue slid over the tip of my cock, licking up the pre-cum before his mouth opened and took in the head. My world shrank until nothing existed except my dick in his mouth. For the fourth, fifth—I'd lost track—time I thought nothing had ever felt as good. Nothing I'd ever done to myself had prepared me for the pleasure I experienced. I closed my eyes and concentrated on his mouth and the wonderful things it did to my cock. He sucked, took me deep into his mouth and teased with his tongue while I made noises I'd never heard before.

I forced my eyes open and looked to the side straight at Aidan's straining cock. I acted without thinking and closed the short distance before kissing the tip of his cock. Curiosity and lust controlled my actions as I took my cues from Aidan. I licked the pearly drops escaping his cock and tasted his slightly salty essence.

He withdrew his mouth and the loss felt almost painful. "You don't have to." I knew he meant the words but I also heard the desire in his voice.

"Shut up. I want to." I put my lips back on his cock as soon as the words left my mouth.

Aidan laughed out loud before taking me back into his mouth again. He led and I followed. Aidan made me feel pleasure beyond anything I could have imagined and I copied his moves, in the hope it would be as good for him as it was for me. I tried taking his full length when he swallowed mine and nearly choked.

"Don't push yourself. That takes practice." Aidan's words reassured me before I had time to worry about failing him. I made a mental note to make him teach me but limited myself to what I could handle. I don't know how long we enjoyed each other like that. He took me to the edge several times only to stop his movements until my orgasm retreated. I mirrored his actions best I could and pride filled me when he couldn't stop his hips from bucking any more than I could.

For the second time that evening my orgasm came first. Lights went off behind my closed eyes, my whole body jerked as an explosion went off in my balls. My mouth never left his cock and when he tried to pull away shortly after my body had calmed down, I refused to let him.

"Lennart, I'm close. Let me go."

I ignored him. I wanted him to come in my mouth, just like I'd come in his. I rejoiced when his cum hit the back of my throat. I swallowed what I could and allowed the rest to escape. Pride swelled inside me, accompanied by another feeling I couldn't begin to put a name on.

For a while we just lay on the bed, resting our heads on each other's legs before Aidan moved around and kissed me. We tasted of each other and the thought made my limp cock stir, much to Aidan's amusement.

"There's no stopping you now, is there?"

I flushed again and tried to turn my head away.

"No need to be ashamed. It's quite a compliment to me you know? And besides, you're having pretty much the same effect on me."

Aidan took my breath away. Every time my insecurities rose to the surface he knew exactly what to say. He lay down next to me and pulled me close until my head rested on his chest. His hair tickled my cheek and I smiled as my eyes grew heavy. While my cock might be up for another round, the rest of my body had other ideas.

Our silence felt comfortable and I concentrated on his breathing until mine matched his. I knew the moment he drifted off and followed him into sleep almost immediately.

Chapter Seven

"This is going to be one hell of a job." I looked around the room and took in all the boxes stacked up against the wall. "There's a lifetime's worth of stuff here."

"Well, do you know how long your grandfather lived here?" Aidan's voice sounded muffled since his head was halfway inside the box he had opened.

"Eighteen years, according to the solicitor." I studied the boxes again. "Okay, maybe it's not that much stuff, considering. But where to start? What am I supposed to do with all of it?"

I hadn't planned on starting this project just yet. In fact, I hadn't given it a lot of thought at all. I'd been too busy getting used to the rest of the house and trying to find my way around the neighborhood to worry about the boxes in the two rooms I didn't need. Aidan on the other hand couldn't understand my lack of curiosity and had been on my case about exploring this stuff since we'd crawled out of bed.

Waking up with Aidan had been an amazing experience. We'd been a tangle of bedclothes and limbs when he'd roused me with a kiss this morning. At some point during the night I'd woken up and before dozing off again I'd worried what we might be like in the cold light of day. I'd fretted about nothing. We'd been good. The shower we'd taken together had been better than good. I knew the fact I had a wet room rather than a more traditional bathroom probably meant my grandfather had been unstable toward the end. I didn't like that idea, even if I'd never known the man, but I did appreciate that it left me with a shower more than big enough for two men to not only clean each other but also have fun while they were at it.

"This box only has clothes in it." Aidan interrupted my thoughts and brought me back to the present and the task at hand. "Do you have something like a marker? We should keep track of what's where for when you decide what you want to do with it all."

"Sure. Give me a sec." As I walked away to find something to mark the boxes with, Aidan opened a second one.

"Oh, wow." I heard Aidan's exclamation when I was halfway back up the stairs.

"What?"

"Come and have a look." He turned around as I walked into the room. "Who are these people?"

I stared at the framed picture in his hands, lost for words at what I saw.

"Are you okay?" Concern sounded in Aidan's voice.

"What? Yeah. May I?" I held out my hand and took the picture from Aidan. I couldn't believe my eyes.

"Who are they?"

"That" —I pointed at one of the men in the picture— "is my dad. That's my mum and I guess that's me sitting in her lap. Which must mean that's my granddad." I didn't understand what I saw. "I didn't know I'd ever met him. My father told me his parents died before I was born."

"Well, you would have been how old in this picture? A year?" Aidan looked at me. "It's not as if you would have remembered if that's the only time you were ever in his company."

"I know. I don't understand why there are no pictures of him or him and me in my father's house. I mean, clearly at least one picture was taken." I'd never felt as confused in my life.

"This whole box appears to be full of photo albums and pictures in frames as well as a few notebooks," Aidan said. "You might discover all sorts of family history you aren't aware of in here."

The thought both scared and excited me. I wanted to know more about the grandfather who'd left me this house, who'd disliked his own son enough to disinherit him. On the other hand, did I really want to discover more grounds for hating my father? Didn't I have enough reasons of my own? Or, what if my dad hadn't been the bad guy in whatever had gone wrong between him and his father? The need to know battled with the thought that ignorance might well be bliss and the longer I thought the less I knew what I wanted.

Aidan's uncanny ability to read my mind sprang into action again. "You don't need to decide now. We could bring this box downstairs and you can go through it whenever you're ready. We'll get on with the inventory for now."

I agreed to his plan and Aidan lifted the box and carried it away while I opened a random box and stared at the contents without seeing them. My imagination ran riot. All sorts of scenarios about the rift between those two men followed each other in my mind. What could possibly have been bad enough to make them ignore each other for almost twenty years? Who had caused the rift and why? Part of me wanted to follow Aidan down, upend the box and find out now. Another part of me preferred the comfort of not knowing and wanted to hang on to it for as long as possible.

I walked away from the box filled with bank statements and other official paperwork and opened the next one as Aidan returned. I would concentrate on these boxes for now and worry about the one in my living room later.

It took us two hours to inspect the contents of every box and organize them. Quite a few had been designated for charity shops. I would ask the solicitor what I should do about all the financial and other paperwork I'd found. The five boxes containing books had been set to the side for me to inspect later. I loved reading and wanted to look at every single title before deciding what to do with them.

"That's the last box finished." I smiled at Aidan. "Thanks for helping me. I don't think I would have done it on my own."

"No problem." He returned my smile. "I quite enjoyed this. But now I'm starving. Any chance of a bit of lunch?"

"Right. Lunch." I grimaced. "I haven't got any more food in the house. We ate the last of it for breakfast this morning. Let's go out and eat. I discovered this nice place around the corner and as far as I know they open for lunch on Sundays."

* * * *

The small restaurant was open and served a wonderful Sunday roast. We took our time eating and talked about all the stuff we'd found.

"Are you going to look at those photos?" Aidan looked at me as if he understood how torn I felt about the decision.

"Yeah. I'll have to. Now I know they exist I won't be able to ignore them." I returned Aidan's gaze and took a deep breath. "I know this is silly but…" I hesitated until he nodded at me. "Would you come back to the house with me and stay while I look?"

When he agreed, a weight lifted off my shoulders. Maybe it wouldn't be as hard to deal with whatever I might find, if I didn't have to do it on my own.

I managed to hang on to my new found peace of mind until we got back to the house. As soon as I looked at the box waiting in the middle of the living room, all my doubts about going through the photos and thus the past, returned. Even with Aidan here, I didn't know whether or not I could do this.

"Why is this so hard for you, Lennart?"

Aidan's question made sense and forced me to put words to what had so far only been a vague feeling of disquiet.

"I want my grandda to be a nice man. He left me his house. Right now I can pretend he did that because he thought I mattered. I don't want to discover he only wrote his will because he hates my father more than me." I fell silent and thought while Aidan waited.

"I can't remember my mother at all and I don't think my father ever cared for me. As long as I don't discover otherwise, I can tell myself I did have one relative who did. I like that idea and I don't want to lose it. Am I even making sense?"

Aidan nodded. "Just start with one album and take it from there. We can stop whenever it gets too much for you or if you don't like what we find."

When he looked at me, the understanding in his eyes took my breath away.

I opened the box and discovered all albums had dates stamped on the front cover. I released a sigh of relief. I didn't have to go through all of them now. I could decide what I wanted to know today and what could wait for a later date. It would have been easy to just look at the older albums, but I knew I'd drive myself crazy if I didn't find out where the rift in my family originated. I dug around until I found an album dated 1994–2000. I'd been born in 1994 and if my grandfather had still been part of my family's life by 2000 I would have had some memory of him. I looked at the album and had to force myself to pick it up.

"Let's sit down and go through it."

Aidan's voice took me out of my thoughts and made me aware I held the album at arm's length, as if it might jump up and bite me. In a daze, I walked to the couch and sat down on the edge. I stared at the cover as if it could answer my questions without me having to look at the contents. I didn't look up when Aidan kicked off his shoes, climbed on the couch and sat down behind me.

His thighs pressed against mine and when he leaned forward to rest his chin on my shoulder, I could feel his heart beat against my back. I continued to stare at the cover, waiting for the courage needed to open it. Aidan put his hand on mine and pulled softly until the album opened and we looked at a picture of my grandparents, as they would have been nineteen years ago. My grandfather looked much the same as he'd done in the picture I'd seen earlier. In this photo he sat next to a bed in which a fragile and ill looking woman almost disappeared.

"That much was true at least." I muttered the words.

"What?"

"My father told me my grandmother died a few months before I was born." I pointed at the picture. "This seems to support that. She looks so small. It is as if she's barely there at all." I felt sad for this woman I'd never known and the man who held her hand. Both of them completely ignored the camera, totally absorbed in each other.

We took our time turning the pages and found more pictures showing my grandfather with the rest of my family, including me. He'd been there for my first birthday and in the picture it looked like that day had been a happy one. When Aidan went to turn the page and move on, I stopped him. I couldn't take my eyes off the image. I had no memories of my mother, and my father had only kept a few pictures of her. This picture showed a happy family, something I had never experienced. The atmosphere I'd grown up in had been cold and often distinctly hostile. A deep longing for memories that matched these images erupted in me. A thought I'd banished from my mind long ago resurfaced. What if my mother hadn't died? Would my life have been different? Would she have stood between me and my father and protected me or would things have been the same, except that I would have had two parents who didn't like me instead of just one?

No amount of looking at that happy image would answer the questions I had, so after a while I did turn the page. We flicked through a few more pictures taken on the same day followed by photos of nature scenes and buildings. It wasn't until we were about halfway through the album that we came across a picture of my grandfather with another man. They stood side by side at a railing on what appeared to be a cruise ship. They had their arms around each other and big smiles on their faces. My world stopped turning as words my father had shouted at me a few years ago rang in my memory. '*You, mister, better man up. I won't have fags in my life. I know how to deal with those who refuse to be real men. I've done it before and God help me, I will do so again*'.

At the time I'd only seen it as yet another of his attacks on me. All my life he'd been finding fault with who I was. He didn't like my voice or the way I dressed. He'd made fun of my hobbies and interests and even ridiculed my red hair. When boys in school ganged up on me and beat me so hard they broke my arm and bruised a few ribs, his only concern had been that I hadn't tried harder to defend myself. And now the reason looked me in the face.

"Are you okay?"

Until Aidan voiced his concern I'd been unaware my breathing had grown fast and shallow. I wiped the cold sweat from my forehead before replying.

"I don't know." I turned my head and glanced at Aidan whose chin still rested on my shoulder. "This explains so much and so very little at the same time."

I turned the pages faster and stared at the two men as they enjoyed life together. They'd traveled far and wide if the photos were anything to go by. Quite a few other shots had been taken here in this house and around Dublin. Every single picture showed my grandfather and whoever the other man had been, happy together. They smiled at each other, laughed or looked at each other with what I thought was love in their eyes.

I looked at the box and the notebooks it still held. I picked one up and opened it on a random page. I stared at the page and the date— *April 20, 1998* – and started reading out loud.

"*The card returned in the mail today. My son obviously meant it when he told me he never wanted to hear from me again and wouldn't allow me anywhere near my grandson. I miss Lennart. He turned four the other day, and I haven't seen him since he was eighteen months old. When Sean handed me the envelope, he looked at me with a mixture of pity and fear in his eyes. He knows how much this situation tears me up inside. My only son and my only grandchild have been torn from my life because I dared to love again. Would it have been different if I'd fallen for another woman rather than a man? I guess I'll never know. I couldn't and wouldn't change Sean or what I have with him. He's made it possible for me to love again when I thought that emotion was lost to me. I know he's afraid I'll let him go to make peace with Thomas. I can't. I need him too much. I can't see myself living without Sean. I don't want to imagine what that would be like.*

"I'm not sure what Thomas' problem is. I didn't raise him that way. How did he end up so small-minded and bigoted? I refuse to give in to his emotional blackmail. I've no guarantee giving up Sean would change anything, but even if it did, I wouldn't be able to push him away. I can only hope that one day Lennart will discover I exist and that he will be curious enough to come and find me. If I live long enough, we may still get an opportunity to get to know each other."

At first I didn't understand why Aidan took the notebook from me and put it aside. I only became aware of the tears running down my face when he wiped my cheek with his thumb. I turned my head and opened my mouth to say something but didn't have the words. Aidan pulled me close until the back of my head rested against his shoulder.

I cried like I couldn't remember ever having cried before. 'What-if' scenarios played through my head. If only I'd known. Maybe if I'd asked more questions, if I'd looked into my background, if I hadn't just accepted my father's words. The more I thought about it, the fiercer the pain became. I'd lived my entire life in a house where I felt unwanted when less than two hundred miles away, somebody had missed me and wanted to know me.

Sounds started to filter through my sobs. "I'm sorry. It's okay. That's it. Let it go."

Aidan murmured the platitudes in my ear and each one hit a mark, making me feel safe and cared for. I cried until I'd no tears left.

"Did you hear that? He wanted to know me. He missed me. And that bastard..." I didn't have the words or the energy to express all the emotions thinking about my father evoked in me.

"Do you think that's the reason your father was so hard on you?"

Aidan's question pulled me up short. Could it be that easy? Had my father hated me because he thought I might be attracted to men too?

"I don't know. Maybe. I can't remember a time he wasn't on my case. I mean, in that other photo it looks as if he was happy once, as if he loved me at some point. But in my memory, he's never liked me." I tried to remember back as far as I possibly could and came up with nothing resembling a happy memory. "How gay can a five year old possibly be?"

"A five year old? What do you mean?" Aidan asked.

"I have a very clear memory of him telling me I wasn't wanted and to go away so he didn't have to look at me anymore. I think I was about five at the time." As I talked, other, successfully repressed, memories tried to push their way to the forefront of my mind but I refused to acknowledge them. I didn't need any more upsets that day.

"Shit." Anger transformed Aidan's features into something I hadn't seen before. "No parent should ever say something like that to a child. Never."

He turned his face toward me and pressed his lips against mine. He didn't ask questions, wasn't trying to seduce me. He let me know he was there for me in a way words could never have expressed.

I lost myself in his kiss for long, precious moments before pulling back. "It hurts." Grief and self-recrimination tore at me. "Serves me right, don't you think? I should be grateful he never got to meet me. At least he never knew how selfish I am. I guess my father was right all along. I am a self-obsessed good-for-nothing. I laughed about the perfect timing of my inheritance yesterday. I didn't want to know who my grandfather was. I'm as worthless as he always said"

"Don't you dare." The kindness in Aidan's tone didn't match the strength of his words. "You don't get to blame yourself for this. You didn't know. Your father went out of his way to make sure you never found out about your grandfather."

"You don't understand. I could have asked questions."

"Why would you have?" Aidan turned my head and forced me to look at him. "Did you ever suspect your grandfather might be alive or that your father could be lying about him?"

"No, but maybe…"

"Lennart, I need you to listen to me. You can't change situations if you don't know they exist. Nobody goes searching for people they think are dead."

I knew he was right, but it all felt wrong. The missed opportunity was too big. It wasn't fair. I wanted to know this man, needed to know who he'd been, longed to hear his voice and laugh and couldn't help wondering if he would have liked me if we had met. I would never know. I could feel tears welling up again, could taste them in the back of my throat but swallowed them down.

"Turn around."

Aidan pushed at my shoulder and didn't stop until I'd complied and sat on his lap, straddling him.

"Look at me."

I raised my gaze, which had been fixed on his stomach, and looked into his kind and caring eyes.

"I've known you now for what? Almost forty-eight hours?"

I nodded.

"You want to know what I see when I look at you?"

I hesitated. Did I want to know? "I guess."

For excruciating moments, Aidan stared at me. His silence went on long enough for me to get worried he might be searching for the kindest way to tell me all my flaws. "When I look at you I see..." he stopped again and tilted his head before grinning at me. "Well, the first thing I thought when I saw you Friday night was how hot you were."

"Yeah, right." I couldn't stop the laugh erupting from my mouth.

"It doesn't matter if you believe me or not. I did. Immediately after that thought it hit me how lonely and scared you looked. But you know what, you didn't run. I knew you wanted to leave as soon as I approached you but you didn't. That's brave, Lennart. Others would have told me to fuck off and leave them alone. You took a chance I might be a good guy, despite your past."

He kissed me. His hand on my neck pulled me as close as I could get and his lips caressed mine. I felt lost when he pulled back and looked at me again.

"Since then you've shown me that bravery time and again. You've shown yourself to be generous and kind" — his smile changed into a grin — "not to mention incredibly sexy."

He pulled me close again and this time his kiss was demanding and hot. His tongue pushed through my lips and I opened up to him, surrendered. I didn't for a moment believe I might be sexy but loved hearing him say it and when he kissed me, as his hands slipped under my T-shirt and stroked my skin, I could almost be persuaded he saw something in me I couldn't see myself.

I lost myself in his kiss and moved on his lap, rubbing my growing cock against the expanding bulge in his pants. I wanted to be naked with him again, feel his skin against mine, his cum on my hands and belly. Just as I grabbed his shirt to pull it off him, a loud dinging noise broke through our labored breathing.

"Shit. Give me a sec."

Aidan reached into his pocket and pulled out his phone. I observed him while he read the message, my stomach clenching as his expression turned hard.

"Fuck. Bollix."

He looked at me with such regret in his eyes I feared the worst.

"Stupid. I'd completely forgotten."

"What?" I asked the question unsure whether or not I wanted to hear the answer.

"My landlord. He's called a meeting at the house tonight to talk to all four of us. He'll be there in about twenty minutes. The others are wondering where I am."

"You need to go?" Panic tried to take a hold of me again as I got up and stepped back.

"Yes. I'm sorry."

We stared at each other and I'm sure he recognized how much I didn't want him to leave, just as I read the reluctance to go in Aidan's features.

"Meet me for lunch tomorrow?"

I tried to smile and nodded my head, afraid all my messed up emotions would tumble out if I opened my mouth.

He brushed his parted lips against mine before stepping back with a resigned sigh. "Great. Come to the shop at about half twelve and I'll take you to this charming place just around the corner."

I stayed silent as we walked to the door and clung to him as he kissed me again before leaving. I watched him as he walked away and didn't close the door until he'd turned the corner and disappeared from sight.

Chapter Eight

The gray skies and drizzle greeting me on Monday morning provided the perfect backdrop to how I'd felt ever since Aidan had left the night before. His text later that evening to confirm our lunch date had made me feel somewhat better, but I'd been lost and restless on my own. I hadn't been able to go back to my grandfather's photos and journals. I wanted to know more about him and his life but it would have to wait until I found myself on more secure emotional footing. I knew many things I would discover while going through his papers would be upsetting and I'd had enough for one day. I also didn't want to do it on my own. Maybe I could just ignore the box until Aidan was here with me again. I'd moved the stuff behind the couch where it now sat, at least out of sight, if not out of mind.

I had a few hours to kill before meeting Aidan and decided to keep myself busy. After a quick shower, I walked to the local supermarket, determined to stock the house with food and drink. Next time I received a guest I didn't want to be left without at least the basics.

I'd no idea what I needed or wanted and threw items in my trolley as they took my fancy. About halfway through the shop, I gave the groceries I'd collected a close inspection and nearly laughed out loud. Apparently there was truth in the saying a person should never go shopping while hungry. The amount of rubbish astounded me but I decided to keep all of it, if only because the expiry dates on the bad foods were far longer than those on the healthy stuff.

I'd walked out of the shop before I realized I should have given this mission more thought. I had a trolley filled with shopping bags and no way of getting them home. I cursed my foolishness. I was sure Aidan never found himself in situations like this. He had a grip on life while I floundered around like a recently hedged chick. As soon as Aidan's name entered my mind, memories came flooding back and I indulged them while I tried to come up with a solution to my predicament. Just thinking about the way he looked at me, of his lips on mine, his hands caressing my body, was enough to make me half hard.

When a taxi dropped off somebody close to where I stood contemplating my bags, I lugged them over then hoisted myself and my stuff into the backseat. The driver grumbled when he discovered the short distance I needed to travel but didn't tell me to get out again. The too big tip I gave him once the ride was over changed his tune instantly.

My thoughts found their way back to Aidan as I put everything I'd brought home away. I couldn't help wondering if he'd like what I'd bought. As soon as the question hit me, I started worrying I might never be in a situation to discover the answer. Regardless of the wonderful memories I had of my weekend with him, I couldn't stop myself from obsessing about all the ways in which I might lose him again. I'd broken down and cried in his arms. Little as I knew about relationships, I had no doubt that was the last thing he'd been looking for in a hook-up.

'You're such a wimp. Real men don't cry. Look at you. A broken arm and sore ribs and you're reduced to tears. I'm ashamed of you. You're no son of mine.' My father's words screamed in my head. I knew I couldn't compare Aidan to my father—they were worlds apart. And yet, no matter how much I wanted to trust Aidan's attraction to me, I couldn't suppress the fear that it was only a matter of time before my emotional outbursts would put him off.

Too restless to stay indoors, I left my house for The Hidden Universe much earlier than necessary. I wouldn't mind killing time in the shop while waiting for Aidan's lunch hour to start and looked forward to watching him while he worked. The skies had cleared enough for the drizzle to stop and the walk into town was quite pleasant. As I neared the shop, I started dragging my feet. Part of me couldn't wait to see Aidan again, another part was scared out of its wits that a night apart had been enough to make him change his mind about me.

I saw him the moment I walked into the shop as if my eyes had been drawn to him by some form of magnetism. I knew something was wrong as soon as I laid eyes on him. He stood behind the till talking to a customer, and from where I stood, I could see how hard he tried to be polite and friendly. The smile on his face looked forced and the death grip with which he held the counter betrayed how tense he was. When his gaze found me, he relaxed for a moment, before a deep frown settled on his features.

I repressed the urge to turn around and walk away again. Whatever was wrong, I needed to know. I'd been looking forward to killing time while waiting for Aidan. I'd planned to spend a lot of time with the graphic novels and maybe bring a few, or more than a few, home with me. I made my way over to the book section of the store and roamed the shelves, but couldn't concentrate on the titles or authors and didn't have the energy to pick up individual books and take a closer look at them.

One sentence played on a loop in my head. *He's going to break up with you. He's going to break up with you. He's going to break up with you.* I couldn't stop my mind from repeating the words over and over again. I knew *breaking up* was the wrong way to describe what I expected to happen. We'd had a weekend fling. People didn't break up after a fling, they just moved on. But it had felt like more to me, especially while I'd discovered my grandfather's secret and cried in his arms. And regardless of what the right words might be, I didn't want to move on from Aidan. I wanted more with him, from him, I yearned to give him more of me, all of me. I fought the panic as it started to build in my body, told myself it made no sense to worry about a situation I knew nothing about. My paranoia proved much stronger than my common sense.

"Are you ready to eat?"

I jumped at Aidan's words and his hand on my arm. "Yes. Ready when you are." I glanced at him. The tension appeared to be gone and to have been replaced by sadness. "Are you okay?"

"What?" He looked at me and shook his head. "Yeah. No. I'm not sure. God it's a mess. Come, I'll tell you what's up once we're away from here."

I didn't know what to make of his words. Had the meeting with his landlord gone wrong? Was he in trouble at work? As we walked to a little coffee shop in silence, I didn't know what to say and couldn't bring myself to ask questions. Despite my worries about what could be wrong in Aidan's life, I couldn't suppress the feeling I might be the problem. Aidan didn't utter a word either, completely absorbed in his thoughts as far as I could see. The longer our silence lasted, the stronger the treacherous little voice in the back of my mind became as it informed me Aidan had to be looking for the best way to tell me he didn't want to see me anymore.

"What do you want?" Aidan led us to a small table in the corner of the cafe.

"I don't really care. Whatever you're having, I guess." I cringed at the petulance in my voice and tried to pull myself together while Aidan ordered sandwiches for both of us.

"So, I told you about the meeting with my landlord?"

I looked at Aidan in surprise. "Yes, you did. It didn't go well?"

"That's one way of putting it." A wry smile appeared on his face. "He wants me out by the end of the week. He has a nephew who needs a room and since, as he put it, the other three lads are a solid unit and I'm the outsider, I need to go."

My mind reeled. Selfishly I tried to figure out what that might mean for us before even thinking about what sort of problems this created for Aidan. "What will you do?"

"I'm not sure. I'll try and find something else but with the rental market being what it is, I'll more than likely end up moving back home for a while." His face transformed again and pure anger flashed across it.

"Shit. I don't need this. My parents don't need this and it's going to make my life so much more complicated. It takes over an hour to get to work from there." He looked away for a moment. "I won't be able to see as much of you either. I'm sorry."

"Is it really that hard to find a place to rent around here?" I thought about the situation in my old hometown. The local paper had been full of rooms and houses to rent every week. When I'd thought about moving to Dublin before inheriting my house it hadn't occurred to me it might prove next to impossible to find a roof over my head.

"Harder than you'd believe." Aidan frowned. "Half the country wants to live in Dublin. There are hardly any rooms available—trust me, I checked—and those I did find asked for crazy rents. I'd need a second if not a third job to afford them. Have you any idea how many colleges there's in Dublin?" He grinned as I shook my head. "Google it some time."

The idea jumped into my head again. The first time it had popped up it had seemed ridiculous. Now on the other hand...

Before I could think myself out of it, I opened my mouth. "You can always move in with me."

Aidan looked shocked. "No. That's not why I told you. I'm not looking for charity. We don't know each other well enough to even think about something like that." He smiled. "It's wonderful of you to offer, but this is my problem. You don't need to solve it for me."

"But it makes sense." The more I thought about it, the better I liked my idea. "I have this huge house and nobody to share it with. We get along well." A rather unpleasant thought occurred to me and I ran with it. "I'm not asking you for anything in return. There are no conditions. If you're afraid of looking like a charity case you could pay toward the bills and stuff." I forced my mouth closed again. I couldn't say anything else. Either he'd accept my offer or he wouldn't.

Aidan leaned back in his chair and stared at me. "You mean that? You'd let me move into your house even though you barely know me?"

His question took me by surprise. Why wouldn't I make the suggestion? Wouldn't anyone?

"Yes. Of course I would. And I think it would be good sharing the house with you. It's on the large side for one person." I didn't say it would be great because I wanted him close. Even if he slept in one of the other bedrooms, I'd still have him and his friendship under my roof.

"If you're sure you're not just offering because you feel sorry for me."

The thought made me smile. "I don't think I could feel sorry for you if I wanted to. You're so sure of yourself and how you want to live your life."

"If only."

He muttered the words but I still heard them.

"Okay. If you're sure, I'd love to move in with you if I can afford to. What do you have in mind for rent?"

I hadn't even thought about rent and didn't want to take any money off him. "There's no need for that." I saw his frown but ignored it while I continued. "It's not as if I have a mortgage to pay or anything like that. If you want to pay your share of the bills and groceries, that'd be great."

"No, I told you. No charity. If I move in with you, I pay rent as well as part of the other expenses."

I wanted to point out to him that he'd be able to give his parents more money if he didn't have to pay rent but bit the words back. If he moved in there would be time for discussions like that in the future, once he'd gotten used to the idea. I just wanted him to say yes. If that meant I had to accept money he couldn't realistically afford to give me, so be it…for now.

"Okay. If that's the way you want it. But you decide how much you want to pay. I've no idea about such things." Excitement about the idea rushed through me. "So, when are we moving you?"

"I have to be out by Saturday." Aidan's face darkened again. "Larry, my boss, has offered to help me move my stuff with his car on Friday night. Will that be okay?"

The honest answer would have been that Friday was too far away for my liking, but I kept that thought to myself as well, and told him Friday would be perfect.

Aidan was a different man when we walked back to The Hidden Universe and so was I. I followed him into the shop and did the shopping I'd been hoping to do before lunch. When I left I'd acquired the start of a graphic novel collection as well as a few Doctor Who figurines. My new life in Dublin was coming together in ways I hadn't been able to imagine. I looked forward to adding the personal touches to my rooms and couldn't wait for the moment I'd be able to share them as well as my house with the man who'd introduced me to all I had been missing in the past.

Chapter Nine

The week dragged, although I did what I could to keep busy. Aidan and I met most days for lunch and once or twice for a pint after work as well. I invited him to stay over at my place a few times, but he told me he needed the time to get himself organized and returned to his soon-to-be-former lodgings every night.

I'd bought ten liters of paint after I left The Hidden Universe on Monday and had been busy painting one of the spare bedrooms cerulean blue. Despite all the time we spent together over the past week, we hadn't discussed where he would be sleeping and I didn't want him to think I'd assumed he would move into my bed as well as my house. I wanted him there all right, but even I, with my lack of experience when it came to relationships, knew we probably needed to spend more time getting to know each other before making such a commitment.

Friday afternoon I stood in the middle of what might be Aidan's room later that day, and turned on the spot. The walls looked well, especially now, with the sun bouncing off them. I'd found curtains and bedclothes to complement the color. Matching wooden furniture that had been here when I moved in finished the room nicely. I smiled. The first room in this house to be decorated had been done up for someone who I hoped would never sleep there.

I checked the time and headed for the shower. I would meet Aidan and his boss at the shop and drive to Phibsboro with them. Aidan had been very reluctant when I'd offered to help him move. I remembered our conversation as the warm water beat down on me.

'There's no need for you to come. I haven't got that much stuff. Larry and I can do it together easily.'

'I want to help. Unless you tell me there's no room in the car for me and your possessions, I want to be there when you move out.' I'd surprised myself with my insistence, but something about Aidan's mood and his reluctance to let me come with him made me all the more determined to get my way.

'Are you sure you wouldn't rather wait for me in your place?' The mild note of pleading in Aidan's voice had almost made me change my mind, but I'd stuck to my guns.

'No.' I smiled to take any possible sting out of my words. *'I'd drive myself crazy waiting. If you arrived five minutes after the time I expected you, I'd convince myself you weren't coming at all. Going with you is the only thing likely to keep me sane.'*

Aidan's deep sigh at my words still tore at me. But he'd agreed. Given his reluctance, it hadn't felt like much of a victory, but I'd taken it.

* * * *

Twenty minutes after leaving The Hidden Universe, Larry pulled up in front of Aidan's soon-to-be old address. The house and street were residential and rather unremarkable. Given the location, I imagined it was a good place to live. Walking distance from city center but in a quiet neighborhood with lots of shops close by, this looked like the sort of rental I would have been desperate to find if I hadn't inherited my house.

Aidan had been quiet on the drive over, reacting only in monosyllabics when Larry or I asked him a question. He was slow getting out of the car and even slower walking up the garden path to the front door. I watched him as he took a deep breath before sticking his key into the lock and opening the door. My stomach clenched and suddenly I wished I'd taken him up on his offer and had just waited for him at home.

I took a deep breath of my own and followed him into the house. I'd no reason to be nervous. Aidan stalked to the stairs and walked up like a man on a mission. I didn't notice the three men standing at the end of the hallway until Aidan was halfway up the stairs. With their arms crossed and closed expressions on their faces, they reminded me of the boys and men who'd tormented me when I still lived in the west. My stomach cramped. The solid presence of Larry behind me kept me going forward when all my instincts screamed at me to turn around and run back to the relative safety of the car.

Aidan had the smallest room in the house. It only held a single bed and a chest of drawers. You couldn't have fitted another piece of furniture in, not even a bedside table.

"Jaysus, man, this isn't much of a room." Larry voiced the thoughts I'd been keeping to myself. "I hope you got on with your housemates. You couldn't spend a lot of time in here without going mad."

"It was okay." Aidan's voice sounded flat and he avoided looking at us. "That's the lot of it." He pointed at two boxes, a garbage bag and a suitcase. "All my worldly possessions. Let's get this done and over with."

Larry grabbed a box and the bag and I took the other box, leaving Aidan with the suitcase. Aidan followed Larry out of the room and down the stairs with me bringing up the rear. By the time I reached the ground floor, Larry had walked out the front door. The three men still leaned against the wall at the far end of the hall and they still intimidated the shit out of me so I hurried to catch up with Aidan.

"Hey, you."

I nearly dropped the box when a voice shouted out behind me.

"The keys?"

Aidan stopped walking so abruptly I almost ran into him. He squared his shoulders before putting the suitcase down and turning around. He took two keys from his pocket and walked the few steps toward the men.

When I thought about it later, I couldn't explain it, but the idea to keep on walking and leave Aidan alone with them never crossed my mind. I stood there with the box in my increasingly tired arms, fear assaulting me but unable to walk or look away.

Aidan didn't say a word when he handed the keys to the man in the middle. I looked at his face as he walked back toward the spot where his suitcase and I waited, and couldn't read his expression. His face was blank, his gaze fixed on something I couldn't see.

We were two steps away from the front door when a voice rang out behind us. "Good riddance to the arse-jockey."

Aidan stopped walking. Even with his back facing me I could hear his breathing getting heavier. I knew I had to be imagining it, but I would have sworn I saw anger vibrating off his tense body. Inside my head, a voice started screaming so loud it surprised me nobody else heard the words. *Keep going. Just walk out. Please don't confront them. It's not worth it. Please don't, please don't, please don't.*

"Aidan, are you okay, mate? Somebody wants my parking spot, get a move on."

Larry's voice triggered Aidan into moving again just when I thought he was about to turn and confront his former housemate. I followed him out on not quite stable legs. That had been too close. I'd felt the hate as if it had been a physical manifestation in that hallway. I could still feel it in my bones, taste it on my tongue and experience the tremors of fear it sent rushing through my veins.

I all but threw my box onto the back seat of Larry's car and rushed in after it. I couldn't get away from this vile place fast enough. I hadn't expected to completely shake the hate when I moved to Dublin, but I hadn't been prepared to come across it in Aidan's life. Aidan, who'd pulled me through so many of my fears. Aidan, who I'd thought of as confident about who and what he was from the moment we'd met. If shit like this happened to someone like Aidan, what sort of a chance did I stand?

The thoughts tumbled through my head as I tried to pull myself together. Nothing had happened. They'd just been words and I would never have to meet those men again. I only realized how selfish my thoughts were when Aidan reached back from the front seat and squeezed my knee.

"Are you all right, bud?"

I covered Aidan's hand with mine while taking a deep breath in an effort to make my voice as stable as possible before answering. "I'm fine." I had questions for Aidan but didn't want to discuss any of what had happened in front of a man I barely knew. Aidan trusted him and Larry hadn't even raised an eyebrow when I'd been introduced to him, but I couldn't bring myself to trust anyone other than Aidan.

Larry tried to engage us in conversation once or twice during the drive to the other side of the river Liffey but neither Aidan nor I was in the humor to engage with him. Thankfully he accepted our non-responses without question and chatted on as if our silence was a normal reaction. Still, the journey couldn't go quick enough for me. Every red light we had to stop for made me more impatient to get home. I needed to be back behind my front door in the little bit of the world I'd come to trust, the one place where I felt safe from everything lying in wait to upset my fragile equilibrium.

Larry whistled when he pulled up in front of my house. "Moving up in the world, hey, mate?" He grinned at Aidan before turning the same smirk on me.

I watched Aidan as he looked at his boss and forced a smile. "Yeah. Moving up to a better place, in more ways than one."

"I'm sorry, lads, but I'll have to drop you and leave. I've got people to meet and things to do." Larry jumped out of the car and opened the boot. He was gone a few minutes later, leaving me, Aidan and his possessions just inside my front door.

"Are you okay?" Aidan barely glanced at me and my heart hurt for him. "I should have just told you not to come. There was no need for you to experience that. The bastards. Why was getting rid of me not enough for them?"

"Aidan?"

He slowly looked up at me.

"Why didn't you tell me?"

"I don't know. I haven't told anyone. What would have been the point? I lived there and although I looked for another room, I couldn't find anything. Telling you wouldn't have changed the situation." He sighed. "Also…" He stopped talking and shook his head. "Never mind."

"What?" I couldn't conceal the frustration in my voice and wasn't sure I wanted to hide it from Aidan. I'd bared my soul to him, shared all my shit and even cried on his lap. And he hadn't been able to tell me he lived with three bullies?

"Your confidence was growing." Aidan sounded defensive. "You were so happy to be away from your father, your hometown and all the bullying you'd endured. I didn't want to tell you it could be just as bad here." He paused. "And there was no need. I had no intention of ever bringing you to that place. Even if I'd gotten on with those pricks, my room would have been too small, and who wants to hang out with their boyfriend while three strangers are in and out of the same house all the time?"

The angry retort I'd been working on as he made his speech died on my lips when I heard the word boyfriend. "You mean that?"

"Yes, of course I mean that. I would never have exposed you to them if you hadn't insisted on coming."

"No, not that." I was afraid to ask. "That other thing you said. The word you used. Did you mean that?"

Aidan looked confused. "Lennart, I'm sorry but you'll have to be more specific. What word do you mean? I used quite a few."

I studied the floor in front of my feet while I wondered whether I had it in me to be brave enough to ask. In the end I didn't have a choice. Not asking — not knowing — would drive me crazy. "You used the word boyfriend." I whispered the sentence and wasn't sure whether or not he'd heard me until I saw his feet approaching mine across the floorboards.

"But you are, aren't you?" The surprise in Aidan's voice took my breath away. He'd thought of me as his boyfriend while I'd been barely able to hope I might keep him as a friend. "I mean, I thought you were." My silence clearly confused Aidan. "If that's not what we are... I mean, if that's not what you want..."

"I do. I am. I mean, I want to be." Relief and anger battled inside me. I glared up at him, balled my hand into a fist and punched him in the shoulder. "If I'm your boyfriend, you've no excuse. You. Should. Have. Told. Me." Every word was accentuated by another punch.

Aidan threw back his head and laughed. Tension left his body and the man I'd met, the Aidan I'd gotten used and attached to, returned. "You're right, I guess." He closed the last few inches between us. "I didn't mean to keep you in the dark. I just didn't want to burden you with stuff you didn't need to know about." He wrapped his arm around my waist and pulled me close. "Forgive me?"

Before I could answer, his mouth was on mine and I had to trust the hunger in my response to his kiss told him how very forgiven he was.

Chapter Ten

"Okay, where do you want me?"

Our kiss had gone on forever and had gotten quite heated as hands explored bodies and sensitive organs connected, but all too soon Aidan decided the time had come to face reality again.

"Wherever you want to be. Come, let me show you something." I suddenly questioned the wisdom of painting a room for him. But, I'd done it and since he would be living here with me, he would discover the work soon enough, regardless of where he'd decide to sleep.

We left the boxes downstairs and brought the bag and suitcase up with us.

"Let's leave them here." I dropped the bag at the top of the stairs before turning to the bedroom on the far side of the landing. "You see. Before you used the 'b' word" — a stupid grin stretched across my face — "I didn't know where you would want to sleep so I decided to get a room ready for you."

A bright blush replaced the grin on my face as nerves settled in my stomach. Maybe he'd still want a room to himself. After all being boyfriends and living together in a committed relationship weren't the same thing. "I mean, this is your room, whether you want to sleep here or not." I opened the door and stepped aside, allowing him to walk in first.

"Wow. You did this for me?" Aidan's smile lifted my spirits. "How did you know that's my favorite color?"

"You've been living in blue shirts since we met."

"I love this room." He turned around on the spot and took all of it in, appreciation clear on his face. "But, I thought I'd be... I might..." He shrugged and stepped toward the door. "Let's get my stuff."

"You want to sleep here?" I worked hard to keep the disappointment out of my voice.

Aidan stopped walking but didn't turn to face me. "I thought I'd be sleeping with you. But it's okay. You went to all this effort and I know this whole thing between us is new for you. I understand you need time to get used to the idea."

"No."

Aidan turned when I said the word. It would have been easier to talk to his back and I had to force myself to not look down.

"I did this because I didn't want you to think I was taking you for granted, or that sleeping with me was part of the rent or something. I..." I struggled to get the words out, knowing I couldn't be upset with him for keeping things to himself, if I wasn't prepared to share in return. "I want nothing more than to share my room with you." I allowed myself to look away as soon as the words left my mouth.

"You mean that? You're not just saying that because you think it's what I want to hear?"

"No. I painted this room because I thought it might be what you wanted but even while I worked on it, I hoped you would never sleep here." Aidan's smile reflected the relief I felt. "I still want this to be your room, though. I mean, I can be hard to live with, I think, and you should have a place where you can be alone, somewhere private."

"Why do you think you're hard to live with?" I opened my mouth to answer him but Aidan continued. "And don't tell me it's because that's what your father always told you."

I closed my mouth again. That was exactly what I'd been about to say.

"Let me be the judge of that, okay?" Aidan's tone had softened. "I'm sure both of us are easier to live with on some days than on others. We'll have to learn to live together and we'll more than likely make a mess of it occasionally. So maybe it's good if I have a room to hide in when I'm in a lousy mood or we're getting on each other's nerves or whatever. But I'd still rather sleep with you."

I couldn't stop myself from grinning. I wanted him to sleep with me in every possible meaning of the word. "There's room for your clothes in my bedroom. We could leave the rest of your stuff here for now, if that's okay."

I'd felt rather foolish when I cleared space in my wardrobe so Aidan's clothes would fit in with mine. It had felt like tempting the gods, but for once I thought the higher spirits might be on my side.

It didn't take us long to get his clothes in the wardrobe and his toiletries in the bathroom. I've no idea what it was like for Aidan, but I felt happier with every single item he put away. Up until a few minutes ago, this house had been my sanctuary — now it felt like home. The thought both scared and delighted me. If things didn't work out it would be hard, if not impossible, to get used to living here without him again.

"I feel kinda dirty and sweaty after the move and that encounter with my former housemates. How about a shower?" Aidan smirked at me.

"Go for it. You live here now. You can shower whenever you feel like it. In fact, you can do whatever you want to do."

"That's not what I meant." Aidan walked up to me and pulled my shirt up. "I was talking about taking a shower together." My upper body was naked before I realized what had happened and he moved his attention to the button on my jeans. "I want you to wash me." His voice went husky and he moved in closer to lick the skin between my shoulder and my neck. When he used his teeth, I whimpered as my cock tried to push its way through my clothes. He had me naked in no time at all and stood back, looking at me with a challenge on his face. "Well, how about it?"

I couldn't move straight away. I allowed him to look me over at his leisure. I didn't think my body was much to look at but I'd started to believe he liked what he saw and I couldn't deny how good his scrutiny made me feel. Warmth blossomed in my chest and my cock grew harder under his gaze.

"I'm waiting." Aidan's voice pulled me out of my happy trance and I reached for his top. As soon as I got him as naked as I was, Aidan pushed me into the bathroom and underneath the main showerhead. The blast of cold hitting my head when he turned the water on made me squeal, and I struggled to get away from it. Aidan laughed and kept me in place, while making sure most of the water missed him until the temperature had reached bearable levels. Gratitude for the wet-room once again filled me. The main showerhead was old fashioned and wide enough to soak two men, provided they stood close together. The smaller nozzles in the ceiling and wall sent sprays of water to other parts of our bodies.

Aidan pulled me close and wrapped his arms around me. "We're good, aren't we?" His question pulled me up short. Until this moment I'd seen myself as the weaker link in this relationship. It hadn't occurred to me Aidan might have doubts and insecurities as well, or that he might need reassurance, just like I did.

"Yes, we are. It's just…" Did I want to say the next words? Maybe we'd done enough soul searching for one night.

"Just what?" I should have known I wouldn't get away with uttering an unfinished sentence.

"I've never been in a relationship before. I'm going to get it wrong. My expectations may be skewed." I sighed while the water pounded down on my head. "What I'm saying is, I'm bound to fuck this up."

"And so am I. There is no right or wrong way to do relationships I don't think. You do what works and that's different for everybody. We'll figure it out." He pulled me in tighter until our bodies touched from chest to knees. "And that's enough of the serious stuff. I think we deserve our orgasms."

He reached for the shower gel and poured a liberal amount in his hands. "Turn around."

As soon as I turned my back to him Aidan's soapy hands were everywhere. They massaged my shoulders, washed my back and spent a long time squeezing and rubbing my arse. When he pushed a finger in my crack and rubbed it over my hole I stiffened.

"Relax. I won't hurt you. I'll never intentionally cause you pain. I promise."

"I know." My body relaxed as I said the words and I concentrated on the new sensations. Excitement replaced fear the moment his finger got bolder and pushed lightly against the muscle. I both wanted him to push harder and feared what it might feel like. When he did apply more pressure a small stab of pain made me gasp before it evaporated and transformed into a pleasure so deep I forgot to breathe for a moment.

"Don't stop."

Aidan removed his finger despite my protests and turned me around. "We're not going further now." He kissed me deeply before continuing. "Shower gel is nice but it's no substitute for lube. Don't worry. We'll get there. We've got all the time in the world now."

The front of my body got washed as thoroughly as my back. My nipples stiffened under his fingers and when he pinched them the sensation shot straight to my hard cock. I wanted to hit him when he skipped my groin after he finished with my stomach and went straight for my legs instead. When he got up from his kneeling position he got a third dose of gel and turned his attention to the one area of my body he'd so far neglected.

One hand massaged my balls while the other lazily stroked my cock. I threw my head back as heat and need assaulted me, nearly drowning myself as a result. It wasn't long before I begged him to finish the job. The need to come was so great and I was so frustratingly close I thought I'd lose my mind. Instead of doing as I asked Aidan stood back and handed me the shower gel. "Your turn."

I took my time with his body, washing every inch of his skin while making sure to inspect every ridge and hollow. I hesitated when I came to his arse before deciding he wouldn't do something to me if he didn't like it himself. When I pushed the tip of my finger into his arsehole the tightness shocked me. *How on earth could anyone fit anything larger in there?*

"Another one, please." Aidan answered the question I hadn't dared ask out loud and I gave him the response he wanted. "Deeper."

I pushed in further and felt him stretch around my fingers. The noises he made were the sexiest thing I'd ever heard and made me even hotter. I stopped imitating Aidan's earlier washing of me and wrapped my free arm around his waist until my hand found his cock. I pushed with my fingers and pulled with my other hand and silently rejoiced as Aidan slowly turned to jelly in my arms. "I'm gonna... Stop... Lennart please I'm gonna..."

I ignored him. I wanted him at my mercy for just a few minutes. I wanted him to come before I did. He'd been looking after me ever since we'd met. For once I wanted it to be about him, not me. His body shuddered in my arms as he came, while his groans filled the bathroom.

I held him while he came down from his high, awed by the realization that whatever I had thought before, this relationship wasn't one-way-traffic. We were in this together and we were equals. Aidan might have more experience than me, that didn't mean I couldn't give as well as receive. My cock was still painfully hard against my belly but I didn't care about my orgasm. It would be nice if it happened but nowhere near as good as having a boyfriend was.

"You've suddenly gotten very assertive." Aidan's words unnerved me until he turned around and I saw the grin on his face. "I think I like the new you."

He reached for the bottle of shower gel again and I had just about enough time to make a mental note to stock up on the stuff before he took my cock in his hand and stroked me until my body screamed for release.

"So vocal." I only became aware of my mouth screaming as loudly as my body when he said the words. "You wanna come, baby?"

"Yes. Aidan, please. So close."

"I know." He slowed his movements, taking the edge off my need to climax. "I haven't decided yet if you deserve it. After all, you completely ignored my pleas earlier."

My mind knew he teased me. My body knew no such thing and thrust into his fist in an attempt to force the issue.

"Please, Aidan. Please I can't. It's too much."

"What? You want me to stop."

I thought my heart would stop beating when his hand stilled around my cock. "No! Whatever you do, don't stop."

I'm sure there was panic in my eyes when I looked at him. He smiled and kissed me long and hard while his hand resumed its movements. My groans got lost in his mouth as he brought me to a long orgasm so powerful it almost hurt.

The water falling down on us had gotten noticeably cooler when he broke our kiss and stepped back. His smile was lazy and sweet as he looked first around the bathroom and then at me. "I think this is my favorite room in your house."

"Our house." I said the words before I'd thought it through and knew them to be true.

Chapter Eleven

I glanced at the clock and frowned. Seven o'clock. Aidan should have been home half an hour ago. I'd learned his routine off by heart over the two weeks we'd been living together. Whenever he worked till six, he returned home at six-thirty. I'd been able to set my watch by his timing. The half an hour he was late worried me.

I scolded myself. There had to be a myriad of reasons why he might be later than usual. Maybe they'd needed him to stay on longer, or he might have needed to buy something on the way home. I walked to the kitchen and checked the ingredients. Everything was ready for the creamy pasta carbonara I'd planned for dinner, the salad had been made and the garlic bread would only need five minutes under the grill. For a moment I forgot to worry and smiled at how domesticated I'd become. I loved cooking meals for Aidan almost as much as he enjoyed eating them.

At half-past seven I couldn't keep myself calm anymore. I'd sent Aidan three text messages. The first had been a short and cheery *'story?'* When it went unanswered I'd typed out a longer one, asking him what time he would like to have dinner at. By the time I composed the last one I was done being funny or polite and had limited myself to '*WTF man*'. That had been five minutes ago and still I hadn't received an answer.

I paced up and down our living room, glaring at the clock as if the movement of the second hand caused my anguish. I tried to stop the thoughts from spinning through my head but couldn't prevent images forming despite my best efforts. What if he'd been in an accident? He might be in an emergency room somewhere and I would never know. I picked up my phone and had my finger poised to call directory inquiries when I realized how stupid calling around Dublin's hospitals for no good reason would be. Instead I scrolled to Aidan's number and waited. His phone went straight to voicemail. It explained why my texts had gone unanswered but did nothing to alleviate my fear.

The logical part of my brain told me his battery had died. The nasty little voice in the back of my mind screamed he'd turned his phone off because he didn't want to hear from me. As always, my personal tormentor won the battle for my attention. I needed a distraction and I turned the cooker on to finish the dinner preparations. When the pasta was done, I added it to the creamy sauce. My appetite was non-existent and I'd run out of busy-work.

By the time half-past eight came around, all doubt had disappeared. I'd lost Aidan. I didn't know why or what I'd done to cause it, but I was sure our relationship was over. I fought the tears threatening to fall from my eyes while I told myself I'd always known this moment would come. Aidan being interested in me had been too good to be true from the start. I'd been a fool to allow myself to believe this time might be different, that Aidan might be able to see something in me that others, including myself, had always missed.

I walked to the couch and sat down, pulling my legs up and wrapping my arms around them. With my head resting on my knees, I stared at the door as if Aidan would materialize in front of me if I just concentrated hard enough. I no longer fought the tears and allowed them to drip down my cheeks.

Shortly after nine, I heard a key in the front door lock. A small sigh of relief escaped me. Whatever had caused him to be late it hadn't been a fatal accident. I'd never known I could be happy to see him alive and well and heartbroken he'd stopped caring for me, at the same time.

"Lennart." His voice rang through the house before he sauntered into the living room. "Why are you sitting in the dark?"

I stared at him as he slowly made his way across the room, swaying a little as he went. He'd been drinking. All my fear and desperation knotted up into a large ball of rage deep in my belly. I bit my lip hard to stop myself from screaming at him.

"Hey." He sat down next to me. When he moved closer to give me a kiss, I turned my head away. He sat back and studied me.

"What's up with you?" He moved in again and wiped his thumb across my cheek. "Are those tears? Why are you crying?"

Something snapped inside me and logical thought went out the window. I jumped up and walked to the opposite site of the room. With my arms wrapped around me and my back firmly planted against the wall, I glared at him.

"You want to know what's wrong with me?" I recognized the shock on Aidan's face when he felt the heat of my anger and ignored his reaction. "I was sure you'd been in an accident. I almost started calling hospitals to find out which emergency room you were in. That's what's wrong."

I hated the screechy quality to my voice. I sounded like a spoiled child separated from his favorite toy and couldn't do anything to control it.

"Hold on. That's nuts. I'm not that late." Aidan's face showed me he'd no idea what I meant or what had caused my anger. "I went for a drink with the lads after work. We do that sometimes."

"It's obvious you went for a drink." Words escaped my mouth without any conscious thought on my part. "You're pissed off your head. You decided to just have some fun, come home and expect your dinner waiting on the table for you?"

Aidan's mellow tipsy mood evaporated before my eyes. Anger replaced confusion in his expression and I knew we were about to have our first real fight. The thought scared the shit out of me, but my anger was stronger.

"Who said anything about dinner? Did I mention the word? Did I ask for food?" With every question, Aidan's voice became more heated. "Did I ever ask you to cook for me? Have I given you the impression I want or need you to do that for me?"

He hadn't of course, but I was in no mood to admit it. "I don't see you ever saying no to it," I countered. "You're happy enough to walk in every evening and have your dinner served to you."

Stop it, stop it, stop it. The voice in my head screamed at me to shut up and let it be. He'd come home. If I shut up now I might be able to salvage the situation. Instead of taking my own advice, I dug a bit deeper.

"Just having your food ready for you at seven wasn't good enough was it? Now you expect me to have it ready whenever you feel like walking through the door?"

Nineteen years of taking the abuse lying down got the better of me and I let it all out.

"I know I'm no prize. I'm well aware how needy and demanding I am. That doesn't give you the right to take advantage of my need to please you." I turned away unable to look at him any longer while I continued muttering words. "I don't even know why I'm upset. Always knew this moment would come."

"What?" I hadn't heard or seen him get up and only knew how close he was when he grabbed my arm and spun me around. "You think I'm using you? Because I came home later than you expected? Is that what you're saying?"

"Aren't you? Everybody else always has. Pretend to like me long enough to get what you want and then drop me if I'm lucky, kick me while I'm down if I'm not."

I'd lost track of myself. I felt like an observer to my personal destruction of the one good thing in my life and still I couldn't stop.

"You know what? If you're fed up with me, if I'm not good enough, don't live up to your expectations, you just say the word. Don't leave me hanging."

I saw emotions cross his face and couldn't read them. Keeping further tears at bay, stopping myself from begging for his continued friendship, took all the concentration and will power I had and I knew without a doubt I would lose that battle within moments if I didn't get away from Aidan.

"Your dinner's in the kitchen. If you want it, you can heat it up yourself — I'm going to bed." All fight had left me. I needed to be alone and get used to the idea that once again I'd lost someone I'd become attached to. I turned and walked to the stairs, hoping against hope he'd call me back but not surprised when I made it to the first floor landing without a single word from Aidan.

Time slowly ticked by as I alternated between lying on the bed, staring at the ceiling, and pacing up and down the bedroom. I listened for noises in the rest of the house and felt some satisfaction when I heard the microwave make its familiar dinging sound. At least Aidan would eat the dinner I'd prepared for him.

As soon as the thought crossed my mind, it hit me that none of it mattered. I'd been worried Aidan might have left me, found somewhere else to live, someone else to be with. It should have been enough that he came home to me. Instead I'd gone out of my way to alienate him further. If I'd set out to undermine myself and the fragile grip I had established on happiness over the past few weeks, I couldn't have found a more effective way.

I stopped moving around, stripped off my shoes and trousers and crawled underneath the covers, hoping against hope Aidan would find his way to the bedroom we'd shared since he'd moved in. The ceiling still didn't provide any answers as I strained to hear what he might be up to. I heard him come up the stairs followed by a door closing. I got up and opened the bedroom door. On the other side of the landing, a strip of light escaped over the threshold of the room I'd painted blue for Aidan. If I'd needed any more proof of the damage I'd done, there it was. I'd managed to lose and alienate him. Calm again, I could admit that his coming home late probably hadn't meant anything beyond him not quite realizing how deep my insecurities ran. I had turned a misunderstanding into a major drama with my unreasonable expectations and accusations.

I softly closed the bedroom door and returned to the bed which felt too big for just me. I crawled back under the covers and closed my eyes. The dream lay in waiting for the moment my guard was down.

I'm walking down an all too familiar street and see them in the distance. There's eight of them and I've no doubt they're waiting for me. Even though I shouldn't be able to see their faces because I'm too far away I recognize the contempt and hate in their features. I know I should turn around, run away, try to find a hiding place where I might wait them out because there is no doubt what will happen next and what the outcome will be. And yet my feet continue their journey, bringing me closer to a fate I couldn't escape then and can't avoid now, one step at a time.

They push me from one to the other as if I were a lifeless toy. Then the blows come, hard and fast from every direction. It doesn't matter where I put my hands, what part of my body I try to protect, they always find a different part to hurt. I lose my balance, I'm falling… I'm falling… I'm falling –

"Lennart. Wake up now. It's over. Wake up."

I tried to move away from the hand on my shoulder and wanted to block the voice. The last time I'd heard that voice it had been used in anger. One thought ran through my semi-conscious mind. *I'm not safe I need to flee, I…*

"Lennart, please wake up. Open your eyes. Look at me."

I squinted through my eyelashes. The bedside light had been turned on and I saw the shadowy figure next to me. My nightmare still ran through my mind and I could almost feel the bruises from the beating I'd endured in my sleep. When the person next to me raised his hand, I whimpered, closed my eyes and wrapped my arms around my head. I had to protect myself from what I was certain would happen next.

The blow I'd braced myself for didn't come. Fingers stroked my hair as a deep, soft voice whispered nonsense I didn't understand. I'd started to relax when I felt the mattress move beneath me. I opened my eyes and panic exploded in my body as the figure next to me moved closer. I lowered my arms and pushed myself back toward the far side of the bed, while getting ready to jump and run.

"Lennart, I need you to fully wake up. You know you don't need to be afraid of me. Please. Look at me. Recognize me."

Aidan. What I'd known on some level ever since I'd first heard the voice at last sank in and I relaxed. Whatever happened next, I knew Aidan would never physically hurt me.

"Talk to me, Lennart. You scared the shit out of me the way you screamed and moaned."

"I'm sorry." I couldn't make myself look at him so I stared at my hands. "I didn't mean to wake you up."

"What was that? You've never had a nightmare before. You sounded terrified."

I couldn't repress a shudder when the images of both the dream and the experience it reflected, came back to me.

"I dreamed about something that happened to me a few years ago."

"I've never seen or heard you like that." Aidan's voice held a note of uncertainty. "Why did you have the dream tonight? Do you know? It's because of me, isn't it? Because I was late and we fought?"

"No!" I reflected for a moment and whispered, "Yes, maybe. I don't know."

He moved slowly when he reached for me, as if he faced a skittish animal with sharp claws. I'd done that. With my fear and my words I'd stripped some of his confidence away, the same confidence that made him so attractive to me.

"Tell me what happened. Did you really think I'd been in an accident?"

I looked at his hand lying between us on the bed. He hadn't felt safe enough to touch me and it broke something inside me. I'd been hurt too often to not recognize the same in somebody else. I moved a little bit closer and picked up his hand, directing my words at it rather than his face when I answered his question.

"I did, for a while. And then I clung to the explanation because I preferred it to the only alternative I could think of."

He twined our fingers together and squeezed softly. "What was the alternative?"

Tears burned in my eyes again and I cursed this weakness of mine. I opened my mouth only to close it immediately. If I said the words, he'd have to react. If my fear hadn't been unfounded, everything would end within the next few minutes.

"Tell me, Lennart. You're scaring me. Just tell me, we'll work it out."

"I was afraid you were fed up with me. I thought you didn't want to spend time with me anymore, that you'd found someone else. A more interesting man than I could ever be, someone less insecure."

"Shit." His one word held more feelings than I could identify.

"I tried texting. Then I called. Your phone went straight to voicemail. I thought you'd turned it off so I couldn't bother you."

"Did it ever occur...?" Aidan stopped talking. "My battery died, Lennart, nothing more and nothing less. I forgot to charge it last night and sometime during the afternoon the phone gave up on me."

I'd never felt as stupid in my life. The thought had occurred to me and still I'd allowed my fears to obscure the most logical explanation, coming very close to creating the outcome I feared in the process.

"I'm sorry." Aidan interrupted my thoughts. "I thought you knew I'm here to stay. I clearly didn't realize how fragile your trust in us is."

It tore me apart to lay it all out for him, but he deserved to know what he faced. "Everybody I've felt close to left or hurt me, Aidan. I'm not used to people staying. When you didn't come home and I couldn't reach you, I couldn't imagine another explanation."

"Listen." The forcefulness in his voice compelled me to look at his beautiful face. "I promise you here and now that if I ever want to leave you, I'll say so. You won't have to guess or worry about it. If it ever happens, you will know. Today is not that day." A shadow swept across his face. "Unless you don't trust me anymore and want me gone."

I shook my head, too choked up to speak.

"Can I come in?"

The question broke something inside me. What had I done? I'd forced this confident man to doubt his every move.

"Please." I lay back down and pulled the covers back. The familiar sagging of the mattress when Aidan stretched out next to me reinforced the hope his words had given me. He lay on his back, with his face turned to me. When he stretched out his arm in a wordless invitation, I crawled closer and tentatively rested my head on his shoulder. When I spoke, I directed my words at his chest.

"It's not that I mind you going out without me. I don't resent you your friends. Honestly, I don't. If I know, you can stay away for as long as you want. " When Aidan sighed, I started worrying again.

"I'm sorry. I wasn't thinking and I should have known better. It won't happen again, I promise. I'll either be home when you expect me or let you know I'm going to be late."

The words to tell him that wouldn't be necessary burned on my lips but I swallowed them back. Maybe there'd come a time when I'd be able to take his presence in my life for granted. I didn't have that comfort yet and was grateful he seemed to get it.

"Give me a kiss."

I lifted my head and pressed my mouth against his. The meeting of lips was soft and almost tentative, as if we'd never done it before.

"One more question." Aidan broke our contact. "Those nightmares. Do you get a lot of them?"

"I used to." Only when he asked the question did I realize how unusual the weeks without interrupted sleep had been.

"I've never seen you go through that."

"This was the first one since you moved in."

"Why?" Aidan asked the question I'd avoided asking myself so far.

"I'm not sure. Because I feel safe with you, I guess."

"You are safe with me." He brushed his lips across mine before continuing. "I'm here, with you. I'm right where I want to be."

He kissed me again and this time he took it deeper. Broken pieces inside me glued back together, shattered peace restored itself. I snuggled closer and allowed his strength to seep into me. I vouched I would learn how to trust as sleep found both of us exactly where we belonged, in each other's arms.

Chapter Twelve

"Here. You've got mail."

I looked at the envelope Aidan handed me and my heart sank.

"Aren't you going to open it?"

"It's from my father." I looked at Aidan as if he might have the answers I needed. "Whatever it says in this letter, I'm not going to like it."

Aidan shrugged. "Probably not. Not reading it is not going to make it any better though. You might as well get it over and done with."

It had been two weeks since our fight and things were good. We'd been tentative around each other those first few days. Aidan had called me several times a day and initially I'd needed the reassurance and taken great comfort in it. After a few days I told him that while I loved hearing his voice or reading his texts while he was gone, I didn't need them all the time anymore. I will never forget the smile in his eyes when he told me he enjoyed those calls and texts, that it had stopped being just about me and had become about both of us.

He'd been late once or twice since then but never without giving me prior warning as well as the option to join him and his mates. More often than not I'd stayed at home, happy to let him have his fun without having to worry about my insecurities. I trusted him and was learning to trust his friends but I knew it would take me a while before I would be able to relax in their company.

The day he bought himself a second charger to leave at work permanently—just in case—felt like my birthday and Christmas thrown into one. Having someone in my life who understood me and put my interest first was a novelty and I vowed I would never take it for granted.

Now I stared at the letter in my hand, certain it would upset the balance I'd recently found in my life. I braced myself and opened it.

July, 2013
Son,
As I told you when you left, I've no intention of allowing you to rob me of the inheritance that should rightfully be mine. I'd expected you to come back with your tail between your legs before today, we both know you're not equipped to look after yourself, never mind a house as well. Since that hasn't happened, I'm writing to inform you that I've hired a solicitor and will be challenging my father's will. All I need to do is prove that he didn't sufficiently provide for me when I was a child and the inheritance will be mine.

You can make it easy for yourself and give me what belongs to me, the gesture would go a long way toward repairing our relationship. If you refuse to be sensible I'd advise you to not get too comfortable in that house. Either way, you won't be there much longer.
Your father.

It hit me like a blow. I'd thought myself safe and now, with his short letter, my father had pulled the rug out from under my feet. My mind scrambled, my thoughts jumped from one direction to another. My breathing got faster until I couldn't catch my breath anymore. Panic gripped my throat and squeezed it tight.

"Lennart, listen to me." Aidan's voice came to me as if through a thick fog. "I'm going to count and you're going to breathe along. In, one, two, three, four. Hold, one, two, three, four. Out, one, two, three, four. Wait, one, two, three, four."

The first time we went through the cycle I thought my lungs might burst. By the fourth time my heart beat started to slow. When Aidan pushed me back against the cushions of the couch I closed my eyes and continued the counted breathing, afraid to stop in case my thoughts would run amok again.

Aidan took the letter from my cramped fingers. I didn't open my eyes to look at him while he read it, I couldn't bear to witness the moment he would realize he was about to lose the house he'd only just moved into.

"What does he mean when he says it might repair the relationship between you two? I thought there was no relationship to repair."

I thought about Aidan's question. Until he asked it I'd been so focused on the possibility of losing my house that line hadn't even registered. "I don't know. We didn't have a relationship. My last year in his house he barely acknowledged me. I mean, we didn't even eat dinner together anymore." A thought occurred to me. "When I left he told me I would never be welcomed back. Maybe he means he wouldn't turn me away from his door if I gave him this house first? I don't know and it doesn't matter. This is my house. My grandfather wanted me to have it and I know my father would never accept me for who I am."

"Seems to me you should contact that solicitor of yours." Aidan's voice was calm and collected.

"I know, but—"

"Don't start making up worst case scenarios until you've spoken to the man. If things were as simple as your dad would like you to believe you would have never had the opportunity to move in here."

I opened my mouth to argue with Aidan and closed it again. He was right. I envied Aidan his calm in situations like this. While I would always jump to conclusions and see bad endings everywhere, he had a far more measured approach.

"Okay. I'll make the call now. It's going to drive me nuts, not knowing."

The phone call with the solicitor lasted only a few minutes and both comforted and upset me.

"Well. What did he say?"

"He said" —I took a moment to collect my thoughts— "that in principle, my father is right. If he can convince the court he wasn't properly provided for as a child, the court may interfere in the terms of the will."

"In principle?" Aidan asked.

"Yes. He also said it would be next to impossible to prove one way or another since my father has been an adult for over forty years. And that even if the court were to change the terms of the will it would probably mean we'd end up having to share rather than one of us ending up with everything."

"That's something at least. Did he say anything else?"

"Yes. He told me to go through all those personal papers and photos we found. He reckons those albums and notebooks will prove one way or another whether or not my father was properly provided for."

"Well" — Aidan smiled — "I guess we don't need to make plans for the weekend. We'll have some investigating to do."

"You don't have to. It's not that often you have a weekend off. You must have more interesting plans." I desperately wanted Aidan to be with me while I went through that box but couldn't make myself ask or expect it.

"Well, I did have plans."

My heart plummeted. "Don't change them for me, please."

"My plans involved spending as much time as possible with this guy I met about six weeks ago." Aidan grinned. "I was looking forward to the two of us hanging out together and maybe doing something we hadn't done before. Investigating your family's history and trying to keep the roof over our heads is definitely something new."

I turned to Aidan and kissed him. I didn't have the words to adequately describe my gratitude but hoped the kiss would get the message across.

An hour later, as Aidan was leaving for work, he stopped in the doorway and said, "You know what, Lennart? Worst case scenario, the two of us will have to find somewhere else to live. I'd hate for you to lose this house and I love living here, but whatever your father does, he can't touch us."

He didn't wait for my reply and left while I sat on the couch and stared at the door he'd just walked through. Perspective was everything and he was, of course, right. Whatever happened next I'd get through it provided Aidan stayed by my side.

Chapter Thirteen

"I don't know. I guess we'll go through the lot of it and see what's there. One way or another we should find answers." We'd had a leisurely start to the day and I'd been happy to ignore the task ahead of us. Now that morning had turned into afternoon, I knew I couldn't postpone the search any longer.

"Nah. We need a plan, be systematic about it. Do you want to go through all of that history or just concentrate on your father's childhood?"

I thought about it. Getting to know my grandfather better would be fun but wouldn't help us find the information we needed to stop my father. All that mattered right now was whether or not he'd been insufficiently provided for when he was underage.

"Let's concentrate on the years my father was a child for now." I opened the box and started emptying it. "We'll put everything in chronological order on the dining table and concentrate on the albums dated between say nineteen-sixty and nineteen-eighty I guess."

The collection of albums and notebooks looked far more impressive once we had them lined up on the table and for a moment I felt overwhelmed. Aidan, on the other hand, had no such qualms and picked up the photo album starting in nineteen-sixty. We made ourselves comfortable on the couch. I nestled myself in front of Aidan, in between his spread thighs, opened the album on my lap to the first page and stared at a photo of a young couple.

"You look like him."

Aidan verbalized what I had realized with something of a shock. If it hadn't been for the fifty-five years between us we might have been brothers. The same skinny — although Aidan would call it slim — build, the same eyes and mouth and, although I couldn't tell from the black-and-white picture, I had no doubt his hair had been as red as mine.

"You reckon that's why your father hated you? Because you look so much like your grandfather?"

I thought about Aidan's question before answering. "I guess that's possible. He did slag me off for my red hair and my lack of muscles all the time."

"Your father looks completely different then, does he?"

I stared at the pretty woman standing next to my grandfather in the picture. "Yes. I guess my father took after his mother. Same dark hair, same eyes and even the same mouth, although I can't remember him smiling like that, ever."

Aidan shrugged. "You know what that means, don't you?"

I had no idea what he meant and told him so.

"It means that your father hating you never had anything to do with you. He took his anger with his father out on you, his child, because you reminded him of the man he'd learned to hate. It wouldn't have mattered what you did or who you turned out to be. As long as you looked like your grandfather you were doomed."

I tried to figure out whether that knowledge made me feel better or worse and came up with nothing.

"From what I've seen and heard so far," Aidan said, pulling me out of my thoughts, "you won the jackpot when it came to genes."

I smiled at Aidan, grateful for the lighter note and returned my attention to the album. I studied the photo again and looked for any signs my grandfather might have been with his wife under duress. Given what I knew about his life after his wife had died I expected to see some signs of reluctance in his posture or face. Either he'd been a great actor or things hadn't been quite as black and white as I thought because the longer I looked at the picture of that young couple the more certain I became they'd loved each other without reservation.

Once again Aidan and I were on the same wavelength. "You reckon your grandfather was bisexual?"

"Must have been, don't you think? Is it even possible to feign adoration like that?" I pointed at the next picture, taken on a summer's day in the countryside. My grandparents held each other's hands while cycling along a country road. Again the way they looked at each other left no room for doubts about the feelings they'd shared.

We took our time, paging our way through the album and found the happy couple again on their wedding day and subsequent honeymoon. The next pictures showed my grandmother with a young boy who looked a little older in each photograph. Far from deprived or mistreated, this child looked spoiled and happy. Pictures taken at Christmas showed trees with mountains of presents underneath. The little boy had gotten a new bicycle whenever he outgrew his old one. In one photo he played with the largest electric train set I'd ever seen. His clothes appeared to be new and clean, and the child—my father—looked healthy.

"This is it, don't you think? If that's a deprived child, I'm a two-headed dragon."

I laughed. "Yes. I think this should be enough. I'll drop this album to the solicitor on Monday. If he needs more, I'm sure he'll tell me." Part of me felt relief the answers had been easy to find. The other part couldn't help being disappointed we didn't need to dig any deeper. I chided myself for my stupidity. Just because we didn't need to look any further didn't mean I couldn't. I had the box. I could look at the contents whenever I wanted.

I turned, gave Aidan a kiss and got up. "I'm going to make us something to eat. I'm starving. Thanks for helping me."

"My pleasure." The look on Aidan's face made me believe he had really enjoyed it. "You cook. I'm going to look through a few of these notebooks if I may."

"Knock yourself out. Just make sure to tell me if you find anything good."

* * * *

"Hey, listen to this."

I looked up at Aidan from the pot I stirred and took in the framed picture and notebook in his hands.

"This is what your grandfather wrote on October 30th 1995."

"When I was eighteen months old." I whispered the words at the pot.

"Yeah, listen."

"*I received a letter from Thomas today. My son has officially disowned me because, as he so beautifully put it, I disgust him and he doesn't want a depraved character like me around his son. He accuses me of having lived a lie all the years I was married to his mother. The lad has no idea. Mary and I were a match made in heaven. She loved me and I adored her. Of course I found myself attracted to men even while we were married. But I never acted on it, never felt the need. For thirty-three years she was all I wanted and needed. He knows how devastated I was when she died. I remember him losing his patience with me when I still couldn't get myself to function six months after the funeral. I can still hear him telling me to man up.*

"*I guess he didn't mean for me to fall in love again. Or maybe that would have been fine if only the object of my affections had been female. I'm not sure what it says about me that I can't give up Sean, even if it might mean hanging on to my family. After his letter I have no problem leaving Thomas behind. It's going to break my heart to give up on Lennart though. I may never see that beautiful boy again. He may never know who I am, or was, or only learn the lies his father will tell him.*

"*I can't walk away from Sean. I've tried to imagine living without him and just the thought of it makes me panic. I'm so sorry, little Lennart. I wish I could tell you how much I love you and how badly it hurts to have to leave you in the past. I hope you'll understand I didn't have a choice if you ever find out the truth.*

"*I'll be severing all bonds with my son tomorrow. I've instructed my bank to settle one hundred thousand Punts in his account. That's the last he'll ever get from me.*"

The tears had started about halfway through Aidan reading the entry. By the time he came to *little Lennart* I couldn't see the food on the cooker anymore for the tears. Once again I tried to imagine what my life might have been like if my grandfather hadn't been forced out of it and came up blank. All I'd seen in the pictures, the little bits I'd read in the notebook, seemed to suggest he was a good man, loving husband and father and honorable person. I couldn't help wishing I had memories about someone like that.

I'd gotten so lost in my thoughts and misery I didn't notice Aidan had moved until I felt his arms around me, and his chin on my shoulder.

"Your granddad was a good man." Aidan's voice was soft and matter of fact.

"I know." I wailed and couldn't get myself back under control. "And I never knew him."

"But you're finding out who he was, what he looked like and what happened."

Aidan's soft voice felt like a blanket being wrapped around me and I surrendered to the comfort.

"I know it's not the same, but it's all you have and the way your grandfather kept all of this, it's going to tell you a lot. You may have never met him, but by the time we're through all this stuff, you'll know exactly who he was."

With Aidan's arms around me I gradually got myself back under control.

"We've done it, haven't we? We've found what we need to keep the house." I looked at Aidan for confirmation.

"Damn right we did. You just get that album and notebook to the solicitor on Monday. I bet there won't even be a court case now we've found this. A letter from your solicitor to your father's should be more than enough to put an end to this madness. Jaysus, your da was anything but deprived. Spoiled rotten's more like it. Even after he'd disowned his own parent."

I nodded but couldn't shake the sadness that had been building all afternoon. My family was a mess. No wonder I'd turned out the way I had.

"But you know what?" Aidan pointed at the framed picture we'd looked at when we first found the box. "I now know exactly what you will look like as you grow older."

"Is that a good or a bad thing?" I smiled, although I felt apprehensive of what the answer might be.

"Oh, very good." Aidan grinned at me. "I've no problem imagining myself with that man."

The way he stared at the photo I had no reason to doubt his words.

Chapter Fourteen

I looked at the table and for the umpteenth time in the past hour wondered whether or not I'd overdone it with the candles and fancy wineglasses. That night it would be two months to the day since Aidan had moved in and I wanted to mark the occasion. I checked the time and saw I had about half an hour left before Aidan would be home. I walked into the kitchen and checked on my preparations. The potato-bake bubbled in the oven. The smell of garlic and cheese made my mouth water.

I prepared the salad and put it in the fridge to keep it cool. At the same time I took the steaks out and left them on the counter. I'd no idea where or when, but I'd no doubt I'd heard or read somewhere steak needed to be at room temperature before cooking for the best result. I wouldn't start on the meat though until Aidan was home.

I walked back to the dining table and stared at the envelope I'd left next to Aidan's wineglass. That had been a happy coincidence. I couldn't wait to see the look on his face once he read the letter.

I checked the time again, any second now. The thought hadn't left my mind before I heard his key in the door. I glanced around again and doubted everything I'd done. The way I'd set the table was too elaborate, as was the dinner, Aidan would know instantly I had an ulterior motive for this feast. And he wouldn't be wrong. I wanted to celebrate our two months as well as the wonderful news we'd received in the mail today. But more than anything I wanted him to fuck me, and tonight, with the aid of a few glasses of wine, I would make it happen.

"Hello the house. Man, something smells amazing."

Aidan sauntered into to the room and I took a moment to admire the man I loved. I hadn't told him yet but the feeling had lodged itself in my heart a few weeks ago. I had no doubt he was all I wanted and needed in my life. And tonight I would surrender all of me to him...if I could find the courage.

He walked up to me with one hand behind his back. He looked from me to the table and back again. "Special occasion?"

My heart sank. I'd been sure he would remember the date too, but apparently I'd been wrong.

He stopped in front of me and looked me over from top to bottom and back again. "You even dressed up for me." He tried to hide it but I could see the grin trying to break through his serious expression. His kissed me long and hard before stepping back and revealing the hand he'd been hiding behind his back. "Happy anniversary, baby."

I looked at the small package he held out to me. It was slightly longer than his hand and wrapped in bright red paper.

"I hope you'll like it." For once Aidan looked not altogether sure about himself. "Go on, open it. Put me out of my misery."

With trembling fingers I took the present from him and carefully removed the paper, I couldn't bring myself to tear off. This present, whatever it might be, deserved my respect and reverence. Once the paper was gone, I opened the box and looked at a gorgeous golden pen.

"I wanted to get you a fountain pen, and then I remembered you're left handed so I wasn't sure how practical that would be so I thought this might be better." The words fell out of Aidan's mouth and he stumbled over one or two of them. "I know you do your writing on the computer but you do take notes on paper all the time and," he had to stop and take a breath, "I want you to do that with a special pen. Because you write special words."

I looked at him completely tongue-tied. I could feel my heart swell inside my chest. I would never know how I'd gotten this lucky. Aidan was so much more than I ever could have wished for or imagined. I'd never dreamed about finding someone like him because I hadn't known people as good as Aidan existed in real life.

I stared at the pen, nestled in its box, and my eyes stung. Love and gratitude battled with frustration. Suddenly my wine and dinner seemed like mediocre treats. "Thank you. I'm going to treasure this pen. It will be as if you're with me, helping me write my books whenever I make notes with it." The sting left my eyes and joy filled me. "In fact, I'm going to take far more notes from now on. I could do my outlines on paper." I looked around. I'd cleaned the room in honor of our anniversary dinner and the notepads I usually had lying on every available surface had been stored away for the night. "I've got to try it, see how it writes."

"I take it you like it then?"

I pulled a notebook from a drawer and turned back to Aidan. "Like it? I love it. It's the best present anybody has ever given me."

The pen wrote beautifully. It fitted in my hand as if it had been custom made for me, and while it was heavier in my hand than the cheap pens I normally used, it flowed across the page with hardly any effort on my part. With this pen I would be able to pretend scenes did indeed write themselves.

"All of this," I waved my hand around the room, "suddenly feels totally insufficient." I wanted to kick myself. A home cooked dinner in return for the most thoughtful of presents.

Aidan looked at me and shook his head before pulling me close. "How often are we going to have this conversation?"

I knew what he meant but didn't think it applied on that occasion.

"I'm not putting myself down. Not this time. I cooked you dinner and I know you're going to love it. But it doesn't compare to this." I looked at the pen again and decided then and there I'd have it engraved with his name. Aidan would be with me whenever I wrote after today.

"Okay. I'm not going to fight you about that. If that's how you feel, I guess that's how you feel. But I'm not about to allow you to diminish what you've done. You planned this." He sniffed the air and grinned. "You cooked potato bake for me, didn't you?"

"Yes, but…"

"Tell me," Aidan interrupted, "how many times did you practice making that dish and throw the result out?"

I looked at my feet before showing Aidan the sheepish smile on my face. He knew me too well even after only two months. "Once or twice, maybe."

"Once or twice my arse." Aidan smiled back at me before turning serious. "Lennart, listen to me. You've been doing special things for me for as long as I've known you. You invited me into your house a week after we met. You painted a room for me when you weren't even thinking about decorating the rest of your house. Every evening when I come home from work you have a dinner ready for me. You clean the house when I work so I can relax on my days off. Everything you do makes me feel special and treasured. Allow me to make you feel the same for once."

I wanted to protest and tell him he made me feel special just by coming back to me every evening but he never gave me the opportunity.

"Do I have time for a quick shower before we eat? I smell like I slept in a dumpster last night, completely out of sync with everything you've prepared here."

"Yeah, go for it. I'll have it all ready in about fifteen minutes or so." In fact, it would be perfect. The chance of me messing things up would be a lot smaller if Aidan didn't watch me while I finished our dinner.

It all came together like clockwork. Just as I took the steaks from the frying pan, Aidan came back down the stairs looking stunning. His tight black jeans framed his strong legs and perfectly formed arse. His tight short T-shirt accentuated his abs and showed me skin whenever he stretched or reached for something. Aidan's dark curls were an artful mess and when he got closer I saw he'd applied eye-liner and blurred it, making his dark eyes smolder and giving him an air of mystery. I forced myself to look away as my cock stirred in my trousers, the resulting contact between naked flesh and metal zip reminding me of my decision to go commando.

"Sit down and pour us some wine. I'll bring in the food." While I walked to the kitchen area, I reflected I'd just as soon forget about the whole dinner and lose myself in those eyes. But I had a plan and had no intention of abandoning it, even if Aidan looked more appetizing than the food I'd prepared.

When I came back with a tray holding our dinner, Aidan had the envelope I'd left next to his plate in his hand. "What's this?"

"Read it and find out." I placed a steak on the plate in front of him before walking around the table and sitting down opposite him. I watched closely as he extracted the letter and read it. His expression changed from one second to the next. I knew exactly what those expressions meant. I'd been through all the emotions earlier that day.

As soon as I'd realized the letter came from my solicitor, I'd been nervous. It had taken me close to an hour to find the courage to open the envelope. Once I'd started reading the letter though, all my tension had disappeared. The solicitor thanked me for my speedy action with the photos and journal and informed me he'd contacted my father's solicitor who'd let him know there would be no legal action forthcoming.

"You've won," Aidan said. "Your house is safe. You did it."

"We won. I could not have done this on my own. Without you I would have given up without a fight." I saw Aidan wanted to argue the point with me and continued before he could open his mouth. "It doesn't matter though. We can stay here. This will still be our home. My father can't touch us. That's the important bit. Now eat. I didn't go to all this hassle just to have it go cold on your plate."

Aidan smiled. "Smart move. You know I'll never let a good meal go to waste."

I watched as Aidan tucked into his dinner with relish. He obviously enjoyed every bite and pride filled me. My own appetite had disappeared though. After dinner it would be time for part two of my plan, and the closer the moment came the less sure I felt about it.

Aidan pushed his plate away with a satisfied groan. "That was heaven on a plate. Thank you." Only then did he notice my plate and all the food I hadn't eaten. "What's up with you? Why aren't you eating? We've had good news," he pointed at the letter, "we're celebrating our two months together and you're off your food?"

"Nothing. I'm just not very hungry." I murmured the words as I refilled my wineglass. Somehow I'd managed to finish mine while Aidan hadn't even gotten halfway through his.

"Lennart?"

"What?" I wasn't ready for this conversation yet. I needed more wine before I'd be able to confess my deepest desire to him.

"Come here." Aidan pushed his chair away from the table but remained seated.

Reluctance made me slow as I got up and walked around the table. My body felt stiff and awkward and my heart beat as if it wanted to work its way out of my chest. Aidan took my hand and pulled me closer until I straddled his lap. He put one hand on the back of my neck and held my head in place while he looked into my eyes as if he might find answers there.

"Are you going to tell me what's up with you? I haven't seen you this nervous since the night I met you, and I don't understand it. This is a celebration. You should be happy, not trying to hide from me."

"Can I have some more wine first?" *You're such a coward.* The voice had been mostly silent for the past month or so but didn't miss its opportunity to reassert itself.

"Not until you tell me what's wrong."

I struggled and tried to turn so I might reach my glass.

"Tell me, Lennart. You keep this up and you'll have me seriously worried."

"It's just..." The inevitable blush crept up my cheeks. "See, I had this plan."

"Okay. What were you planning on doing?"

I didn't want to say it out loud and squirmed on his lap. The movement resulted in my crotch rubbing against his and despite my nerves, desire rushed through my veins and grew stronger when Aidan moved his hands to my thighs and forced me to stay close to him.

"I wanted to seduce you."

"Seduce me? Why would you want to do that? Don't you already have me?" Aidan's confusion was clear in his voice.

I fought with myself. I had to find a way to explain myself to him. How hard could it be? What was the worst thing that could happen? The moment I asked myself the question I wanted to chicken out. I would be devastated if I made the suggestion and Aidan rejected it, rejected me.

"Never mind." I forced a smile on my face and hoped Aidan would let it go. "I was just being silly. Ignore me."

"Don't do that." An undertone of steel had crept into Aidan's voice. "Don't tell me there's nothing going on when it's obvious something is bothering you."

"It's not important." I could feel my panic levels rising and tried to get up again, but Aidan's tight grip on my thighs kept me a prisoner on his lap.

"Lennart, just tell me. I hate it when you go all nervous and secretive on me. You are worrying me now. The longer you stay quiet, the bigger this — whatever it is — will get."

I had no idea how it had happened but I'd managed to get myself caught between a rock and a hard place. If I told him what I wanted, I risked rejection. If I kept my secret, I would at the very least disappoint Aidan and spoil a special evening. I didn't even want to think about what the worst-case scenario might look like.

"I had this idea." I took a deep breath and tried again. "I wanted to seduce you…" God this was hard. "I want you to make love to me." As soon as the words left my mouth the floodgates opened and others followed. "I want to feel you inside me. I need to know what that feels like. I want you to make me yours, completely."

I held my breath as I waited for Aidan's reply.

"But you are mine. You're my boyfriend, aren't you?"

And there it was. I'd gambled and lost. Tears stung my eyes but I managed to blink them away. "Why not? Why don't you want me? Tell me what I need to change so you will want all of me."

"No, baby. You don't understand." I thought I heard an edge of desperation in Aidan's voice. "Look at me, please."

It took a lot of effort to raise my gaze and look into Aidan's eyes. I feared rejection and maybe condescension, but encountered compassion instead.

"It has nothing to do with me not wanting you." Aidan looked away for a moment as if he too had to find the courage for his next words from somewhere. "You have no idea how badly I want you." Heat and lust rolled off his tongue as he said the words.

"Then…what?" My fear had transformed itself into confusion. "If we both want it, what's stopping us? Why are you holding back? I even went and bought condoms today." Aidan had introduced me to lube soon after we'd first met, but we'd never even talked about the need for protection.

The blush creeping up on Aidan's cheeks took me by surprise. Not a lot of things flustered him.

"It's the one thing I've never done before." Aidan spoke so softly I had to strain to hear him.

I stared at him as Aidan looked away. "You've never gone the whole way with a man?" Whatever I'd expected, that hadn't been it.

"I have, but I've never topped."

Relief flooded me, and my body relaxed. This wasn't about me. Aidan rested his forehead against my shoulder and continued talking in that quiet voice.

"What if I get it wrong? The first time is hard. I know. It's gonna hurt no matter how careful we are. What if I spoil it for you? Your first time should be special, not an experiment."

Our roles had reversed for once and I couldn't stop the smile from spreading across my face.

"Aidan, look at me." It was the line he always used with me whenever my insecurities got the better of me. His reluctance when he looked up at me reminded me of my usual behavior as well. "I kinda like that."

"You like what?"

"I think it's great it would be a first for both of us. I like that we'll be discovering this together."

"You don't understand." Aidan's voice got louder as frustration pushed embarrassment into the background. "It's going to hurt. I remember the pain and trust me, if the first time hurts badly enough it becomes next to impossible to go back for seconds."

"I realize that." The first time Aidan had pushed a finger all the way inside me had been almost enough to make me rethink anal play. Until my body got used to it and pleasure erased all memories of discomfort. "But I trust you. I know you'll take it slow, like you do with your fingers. I also know you will stop if I ask you to. I have no doubt there's a greater risk of you being too careful than of you pushing me too far."

"Are you sure you wouldn't rather fuck me?"

"Abso-fucking-lutely." Aidan's question took me by surprise.

"How can you be so sure about that?"

"Because that's not what I visualize when I fantasize about the two of us together. In none of my dreams have I topped you. It is always you fucking me, never the other way around."

Then it hit me. "Shit. I'm sorry. Do you..." I didn't want to ask the question but opened my mouth anyway. "Were you hoping I would top you?"

"No." At last some of the tension left Aidan's body. His grip on my thighs became less tight and soft strokes over sensitive skin sent shivers down my spine. "My dreams pretty much match yours. But I don't like my lack of experience. I don't want you to be my training ground."

I bent forward and kissed him. "Don't worry about it. I trust you. It's like this whole relationship thing—we'll figure it out together. Besides...," I smiled in an attempt to take some of the tension out of what should have been a romantic situation. "The alternative is the stuff of nightmares."

"What do you mean?" Aidan asked.

"I really don't want you to go and practice on someone else first." I kissed him again before he could respond.

As Aidan deepened the kiss I sensed his lingering doubts, but I could feel his cock growing against my own half-hard dick.

I broke our kiss and pulled his shirt over his head and stroked his chest with my hands. I loved the feeling of his chest hair and would never get enough of seeing his nipples stiffen as I brushed over them and pinched lightly.

"No." He grabbed my hands and pulled them away from his chest. My heart sank. He wasn't ready. The thought brought a small smile to my face. Who would have thought me, the novice, would be unable to convince Aidan, the one with experience, to take that last step.

"If we're going to do this" — Aidan sounded breathless — "we're going to do it in comfort, in bed."

Chapter Fifteen

As soon as we'd made it to the bedroom he pushed me up against the wall and kissed me until I thought my knees might buckle. While I tried to catch my breath he peeled my clothes off me one at a time, caressing skin wherever he exposed it. He hummed in appreciation when he unzipped my jeans and discovered I'd neglected to put on boxers.

He knelt in front of me to take off my shoes and jeans and stayed there. He drove me crazy as he sat on the floor, unmoving, his mouth so close to my cock I could feel the caress of his breath every time he exhaled. I wanted to push forward, present my cock to his lips but couldn't bring myself to break the moment.

When he did take my cock in his mouth I groaned out loud. Between the heat of his mouth, his lips softly sucking, and his tongue teasing the tip I feared I might lose it there and then. He took me deeper and sucked me hard until I wanted to scream. I moved my hips and he stilled. I rejoiced as he took every thrust into his mouth as if it was a present. His tongue, the suction and the moistness of his mouth drove me wild.

Just when I thought I couldn't hold back anymore he grabbed my hips and stopped my movements. He slowly drew his mouth off my cock, taking his time and licking his way around the twitching length before letting me go and leaning back. "Get on the bed." I had never heard anything hotter than the need in his voice when he spoke those simple words.

I stretched out on the bed and looked at the man I'd fallen in love with. I admired his body as he stripped off the rest of his clothes. His gaze never left my body, making me squirm in front of him.

"Grab the lube and one of those condoms you so optimistically bought." His voice left me in no doubt he wanted to take this next step as much as I did, despite his reservations. I reached over and opened the drawer in the bedside table. I'd made sure to leave both items in front and turned back with them in my hand almost instantly. I gave them to Aidan and watched as he opened the package and stretched the condom over his hard cock. Uncertainty washed over me. Surely he didn't plan on just pushing into me. I wanted him, but I'd imagined there'd be lots of prep before he'd…

"Stop worrying. I know what you're thinking." He squeezed a liberal amount of lube on his fingers as he continued talking. "By the time you're ready for me my hands will be so covered in this stuff I won't be able to deal with a condom anymore."

I exhaled loudly and my cock, which had deflated as my anxiety took over, reasserted its presence.

"You're so beautiful." Aidan murmured the words as he joined me on the bed. He spread my legs and knelt between them. His clean hand stroked across my chest, teasing my nipples until they were hard pebbles. As he leaned forward to kiss me I felt pressure against my arsehole. His finger pushed through the tight muscles as his tongue forced its way between my lips. I'd grown to love this first penetration over the past weeks. The initial burn still took me by surprise but rather than scare or hurt me, it now only enhanced my excitement. His tongue and finger moved in and out of me in unison until I couldn't keep still anymore and lifted my arse, trying to get more from him, more stretch, more penetration and more possession.

He took forever. Pleasure started to resemble heated frustration when he added a second finger, eliciting a loud and enthusiastic groan from deep inside me.

"Needy." I loved his teasing as much as it drove me crazy. "Let's see if we can't get you needier." He turned his hand on the next penetration and hit me just there.

"Please. More. Please." Anticipation combined with his expert teasing drove me wild. Aidan wouldn't be rushed though. He pumped his fingers, spread them and continued to stretch me wider. And through it all he made sure to hit my prostate on and off, keeping me on edge but never bringing me close enough to find release.

A third finger stretched me almost beyond the point of pleasure and Aidan instantly noticed my reaction.

"If it hurts too much you let me know and we stop."

"No. I want this."

"Lennart, listen to me. There's no hurry. It doesn't matter if we do this tonight, tomorrow, next week, next year or never. We're together. I'm not going to hurt you and pretend it makes us closer. If it's not good for both of us it's off the cards."

I wanted to argue with him but couldn't deny the relief his words brought me. I wanted to feel him inside me. I'd no doubt it would be the closest I could ever feel to him. But I couldn't deny the idea scared me as well.

His cock was so much bigger than even three of his fingers.

"Promise me or this ends here." Aidan's expression left no room for doubt about his seriousness.

"I promise. If it hurts too much I'll let you know." He'd kept his fingers inside me and wiggled them as we talked. The painful edge dissipated and the pleasurable burn I'd come to love returned. I moved my arse in encouragement and a spark of pride lit up inside me when a satisfied grin appeared on Aidan's face.

I hadn't expected the stab of sadness I experienced when Aidan withdrew his fingers. The emptiness appeared much larger than his fingers had felt inside me, and I couldn't stop myself from pleading with him again.

"Please, Aidan. Please, love. I need you. I need this."

"I know. It would be easier if I turned you on your stomach but I need to see your face." He moved closer to me and I could feel his sheathed cock rubbing against mine. "Patience. Slow and easy does it."

He squirted more lube on his hand and rubbed it on his cock in slow and thorough strokes. I watched, mesmerized by the sight and torn between anticipation and fear. The heady combination left me hotter and needier than I'd ever felt.

"Grab your legs and pull your knees toward your chest. Expose yourself to me." Despite his patience he couldn't keep the hunger out of his voice as I complied.

When the tip of his cock broke through the muscles guarding my arsehole I had to close my eyes. It burned beyond anything I'd experienced before. Even the first time he'd pushed a finger inside me hadn't been as intrusive. He stilled, and when I opened my eyes I saw concentration and uncertainty on his face.

I felt torn between pushing away from him and bearing down, getting him inside me and the whole experience done and over with. Pleasure and pain fought a ferocious battle inside my body and my mind and I surrendered to it. I'd wait it out until both made up their mind about how they felt about this experience.

I assume my feelings were visible on my face. Aidan studied me, and the moment the pleasure I felt exceeded the burn he pushed in a bit deeper.

"Talk to me, Lennart. Tell me what you feel." Every word sounded like a struggle, a master feat of restraint on Aidan's part.

"Don't know. Too much. Not enough. It hurts and it's good."

With endless patience he pushed himself deep inside me, inch by very slow inch. The transitions from almost unbearable burn to pleasure kept me securely on edge. He kissed me long and hard when all of his cock had found its way inside me.

"God, you're so tight. I never thought it could feel this good." For the first time since we'd started I heard no trace of uncertainty in his voice. His need further ignited mine and I involuntarily moved my body. He rewarded me with a long and deep groan.

"You okay?" He searched my face for signs of discomfort.

"Yes. Please, just move."

He captured my mouth in a long, harsh kiss again before withdrawing all but the tip of his cock from my arse. He didn't pause on his second penetration. Slow but steadily he pushed his way into me before withdrawing again and repeating the action. I could only lie there and take it. The burn and stretch still kept me teetering on the verge of wanting to tell him to stop but with every push the pleasure became stronger and the discomfort less.

"Harder." I took both of us by surprise when I groaned my demand. I gazed at him through half closed eyes and recognized the restraint he forced upon himself. "Please. More."

"God, man."

Aidan mesmerized me. I fixed my gaze on his face and drank in the moment he allowed his feelings to take control of his body. His movements became more forceful and every penetration brought us closer together.

My cock had gone limp when he first entered me, but grew back to full erection as pleasure made discomfort a distant memory. When Aidan grabbed my hips and angled my body differently so that his cock hit my prostate I closed my eyes, lost in a mind-blowing sensation.

"Aidan, I need... Please." I didn't know what I wanted or needed but thankfully Aidan did.

"Touch yourself. I want to feel you come."

I wrapped my hand around my cock and stroked myself with a desperation I'd never felt before. Lust and heat took over my senses. I was his. I was pleasure. His cock hit my prostate and my strokes matched his rhythm. My stomach muscles tensed and my balls drew up as I teetered on the edge of release. When I came my arse pushed off the bed in an effort to get even closer to Aidan. As I clenched and unclenched around his cock he felt even bigger than before and it drew my orgasm out. Cum spread over my hand and stomach and kept coming long after I thought I should be empty.

"Lennart. Oh God you're so hot, so beautiful." His movements became erratic before I felt his cock expand in my arse. I forced my eyes open and reveled in the sight of Aidan's ecstasy.

Just when his cock in my arse started to get uncomfortable he withdrew, leaving me feeling empty. When he pushed himself up and off the bed a deep sense of loneliness settled on me, which lasted until he'd returned from the en suite without the condom and with a washcloth.

He knelt on the bed beside me and cleaned my stomach and chest with tender strokes, before turning his attention to my sticky hand. I closed my eyes and got lost in his ministrations. When he kissed me I passively received his lips and tongue. My overwhelmed body and brain wanted to submit to the delicious tiredness spreading through my limbs.

"I love you." The words escaped and shocked me back into wakefulness. I'd had no intention of saying the words and knew it was too soon. The silence greeting my words confirmed that feeling.

"Look at me." The tenderness in Aidan's voice took my breath away and yet I had to force myself to open my eyes. I didn't want to see pity in his, I didn't want to hear his reasons why he couldn't say the words back to me even though I knew I'd put us in this situation.

I didn't see pity in his eyes when I met his gaze. If I had to describe what I saw I'd call it wonder. "You love me, do you?" His sweet smile tugged at my heart.

"I do, but forget I said it."

"Why would I want to forget you told me you love me?"

I swallowed and thought hard about how I wanted to phrase my next words. "It's too soon, isn't it? You're going to tell me we don't know each other long or well enough to have feelings like that." I wanted to look away but his gaze had me trapped as efficiently as if his hand held my face in place. "I don't want you to feel you have to say those words to me. Just forget it, please."

"I'll never say anything to you just because I think it's what you want to hear." Aidan's voice and face had grown serious. "When I was inside you and saw and felt you stretch to accommodate me, it made sense of something I've been thinking about for a few weeks. I've never told any man I loved him because I don't think I ever have."

I'd been expecting the words and yet my heart and mood both dropped.

"I love you Lennart." My heart skipped a few beats when I heard those words, the shortest sentence with the deepest meaning. "I don't know when my feelings changed from happy to be in your company to needing to be with you. I'm not sure I recognized it as love until you said the words first. But I've no doubt. Here's where I belong. You are whom I'm supposed to be with. Hey, don't cry."

I couldn't help it. Between the emotional rollercoaster I'd experienced while he made love to me, my slip of the tongue and his beautiful and clearly heartfelt words, my equilibrium shattered. Tears trickled from my eyes and down my cheeks to the covers beneath my head. Aidan stroked my cheek with his thumb before putting the digit in his mouth and sampling my emotional outburst.

He pulled me close and I rested my head on his shoulder. I had no more words. My mind didn't want to hold thoughts anymore. My arse still felt used and stretched. I'd no doubt I'd still be feeling the effects of our first time tomorrow and welcomed the thought.

I felt safe and at home in his arms and allowed myself to drift off while the words rang through my mind. *He loves me. He loves me. He loves me.*

Chapter Sixteen

The cursor flashed on my screen. I'd entered my details and password. Just one click on the 'ok' button and I'd know. I wondered how many other teenagers in Ireland were spending their morning like me, facing this September ritual, torn between wanting to know and fearing what they might find.

I'm not sure what made me so reluctant. Whatever I'd see once I went in wouldn't make a difference to my life. Besides, I knew I'd done well. All that remained to be revealed was how well.

I'd left Aidan asleep in our bed. He shouldn't have to get up early on his days off and this wasn't exciting enough to spoil one of his rare opportunities to linger under the covers.

I stopped procrastinating and clicked the mouse. The result appeared on the screen and I stared at it. Five-hundred-and-eighty-five points out of a possible six-hundred-and-twenty five, it was a great score.

"Wow."

I hadn't heard Aidan come down the stairs and his presence behind me took me by surprise. I smiled.

"Yeah. Not bad and more or less what I expected."

"Jaysus, man, what's wrong with you? Most people would kill for a result like that. A little excitement wouldn't go amiss."

Aidan's words hit home.

"You're right. I didn't mean anything by it." I stopped to think. Maybe Aidan had hoped to go to college and been stopped by lack of sufficient points. I could only imagine how hurtful my reaction must have been for him in that case.

He gently squeezed my shoulders and I groaned. Tension I hadn't been aware of disappeared under his touch.

"I didn't do too bad myself you know. I walked away with just under five hundred points. A lot more than I expected."

"But you didn't go to college." I didn't ask since I knew the answer but I'd never asked why he didn't go on to third level education.

"No. I'd signed up for an art course thinking I might be interested in animation. I got accepted too." Aidan paused as if lost in thought. "But I landed the job with The Hidden Universe that summer and loved it. I didn't want to spend four years balancing work and study without any time to live so I didn't take my place and stayed in the job."

"Do you regret that?" I needed to know. I'd made up my mind not to go to college. I hadn't even applied for a course but suddenly worried whether I'd kick myself for that decision a few years from now.

"Regret it? Not at all. I still love that job and there's nothing stopping me from drawing whenever I want. And if I ever change my mind I can always go back to school as a mature student. What about you?"

"Me, what do you mean?"

"Don't you want to go and study? I could see you taking English. Might come in handy with the writing and all."

"No. I didn't apply for any courses. I couldn't wait to get out of school and away from the forced proximity to other students. Fourteen years was more than enough for me." I flinched when I heard the vehemence in my voice.

Aidan looked at me for a moment. "It was only a question."

"I know." I sighed and searched for an explanation he might understand.

"If your only choice was to either move back in with those pricks you used to live with or sleep on a bench in the park, what would you do?"

He stared at me and I saw realization dawn on his face. "I'd pick the bench, in a heartbeat." His face darkened. "I wouldn't go back there if it was the last roofed building in Dublin. I'm still not sure why I stayed as long as I did, except that I couldn't see a way out."

"Exactly." I nodded. "I'm not saying I'll never go to college or even that I'll always be weary of groups of people but back then..." I shuddered. "Just the idea of opening myself up to the risk of being picked on again was enough to give me palpitations."

With the mention of those palpitations came the memories. I remembered coming home from school in tears day after day those first few years of primary school and begging my father to allow me to enroll somewhere else. My father's reaction to my begging had been unsympathetic to say the least. He'd consistently put the blame on me, and had always told me to man up, to make a stand against the bullies.

'If you stopped being such a wimp, they'd leave you alone. Fight back. Give them a black eye. That'll teach them.' I didn't think I'd ever be able to forget his voice or the contempt in it.

"I remember…" I stopped, not sure I wanted to share this memory with Aidan.

"Yes. Don't stop."

"When I was fifteen, a gang of eight boys waited for me halfway between school and home. I saw them from a distance but I didn't have an alternative route to take. They blocked the road so I had to stop."

I stared at Aidan without really seeing him while I wondered why I felt the need to drag this memory from the depths where I'd buried it, when only a few weeks ago, after my nightmare, I hadn't been able to make myself tell him about it.

"Go on, love."

"At first they just pushed me around and called me names." As I remembered, the confusion I'd felt at the time came back to me. "They kept on calling me faggot and gay and I didn't understand. I hadn't quite figured it out for myself yet and had no idea why they would label me like that."

I could see it all in my mind. By that time I'd learned not to cry and not to fight back. I knew my best chance of getting out of the situation in one piece lay in ignoring them as best I could.

"That day the strategy didn't work. The more I refused to react, the more frustrated and violent they became until they pushed and beat me hard enough to throw me to the ground. I landed awkwardly and broke my arm."

I hated the emotion I could hear in my voice, resented those boys for still being able to get to me four years later. And the worst part of the tale, for me at least, hadn't been told yet.

"I dragged myself home and waited for my father to come back from work. I knew something was wrong but had no way of getting myself to a doctor or hospital and knew better than to disrupt his day. When he came home, my arm had swollen to twice its normal size and was black and blue. My father didn't want to know. He told me he had a meeting to attend and no time to take me to be checked out. He..." I paused to gather my thoughts and keep my emotions under as much control as I could muster. "He was quite calm while he told me to stop being a baby and that he hoped this meant I would start defending myself in the future."

I halted again. Even though I detested my father, it still hurt to have to admit how much of a bastard he'd been. "He didn't take me to the hospital until two days later."

"What?"

I smiled. One of two good things in the middle of that nightmare had been watching my father squirm his way through awkward excuses when the hospital staff asked how I'd broken my arm and why he'd waited so long before bringing me in for X-rays.

"I had to stay in hospital for an operation and had pins in my arm as well as a cast for weeks." I twisted my arm and showed Aidan the faint scars on my arm he'd missed in his explorations of my body so far. My heart melted when he kissed each of them with reverence.

"It wasn't all bad though. Thanks to the cast, those bullies left me alone for about eight weeks. I think they were afraid I might name them."

"You didn't report them?" Disbelief rang in Aidan's voice.

"No. With my father refusing to complain to the school and everybody there bullying me to some degree, it seemed easier to just stay quiet. Even if those eight boys had been punished, others would have taken their place or they'd have turned even more violent once attention had shifted away from them."

Aidan sighed. "Okay, I get that. It's not right though. Makes me want to get on a train and beat the shit out of those people...your father included."

"That makes two of us." I smiled. "But I've left them behind me now. This is a new life and I want to leave the old one in the past. I'll never forget those years but I don't want to give them any more power over me."

His lips brushed mine before he deepened the kiss. "We need to celebrate those results. How about we go out for a big and decadent breakfast and then make a day of it?"

Chapter Seventeen

"How do I look?" I glanced at myself in the mirror one more time before turning to Aidan who gave me a bemused smile.

"As hot as ever."

"That's not what I mean and you know it." I glared at him for making fun of me while I could barely keep a handle on my nerves.

"Lennart, will you stop. Don't turn this into a huge and momentous event. We're having them over for dinner, that's all."

"I know." I sighed and turned to the mirror again. "But, do I look okay? Maybe I should get that white shirt. Are you sure I shouldn't wear a tie?"

I watched as Aidan's reflection shook his head and bit on his lips in an effort not to laugh.

"It's not funny. I'm meeting your family for the first time and it's freaking me out. What if they don't like me?"

Aidan's face turned serious. "Why would they not like you? What's to dislike?"

"That's how it's always been." I looked away and took a deep breath before continuing. "I want to believe you, but what if you're wrong?"

He crossed the room and turned me away from the mirror when he arrived behind me. "Listen to me. They're not coming to judge you."

I opened my mouth to protest but he beat me to it.

"Of course they're curious about you. I've never lived with a boyfriend before. This is the first time I've ever wanted to introduce any of the guys I dated to my family. So yes, they want to know who you are and why I think you're so special. All they want is for me to be happy. When they see how happy I am with you, they'll like you. Don't over think this."

"Easy for you to say." I muttered the words under my breath, more out of habit than from real fear. I was nervous but nowhere near as panicky as I'd expected to be.

"Come," Aidan pulled me away from my reflection. "We'd better make sure everything's ready. They'll be here in about fifteen minutes."

My heart skipped a beat at the reminder but I followed him downstairs. As we descended the stairs, the aroma of the lasagna in the oven became stronger. I glanced at the timer as we walked through the kitchen and saw it should be done in about half an hour. Provided Aidan's family didn't arrive late, the timing would work out perfectly.

For the first time since I'd moved in, we needed most of the dining table. Seven settings had been laid out. Wine and water sat waiting on a sideboard. Excitement battled with worry as I acknowledged we were as ready as we'd ever be.

We'd had visitors before, friends of Aidan's and some of his colleagues dropped in quite regularly. I never turned those occasions into formal affairs though. More often than not we would end up ordering pizza and drinking beer while listening to music, watching a DVD or playing computer games. I didn't worry about those visitors, hadn't been given the opportunity to think about it much. One evening Aidan brought a few of them home from work with him and that had been that. And, I had to admit that none of them seemed to hate me. I'd no idea whether they liked me or not but couldn't deny they'd always treated me exactly the same as they did Aidan.

I sighed. While I was glad they appeared to have no problem with me, I'd never worried about their opinion. Aidan's family on the other hand…

"You're doing it again." Aidan wrapped his arm around my waist and pulled me close.

"What?"

"Worrying. Will you ever stop? What's the worst possible thing that could happen?"

"They'll hate me."

"And why"—Aidan smiled—"would that be so bad?"

I opened my mouth to answer him and closed it again.

"That's right. You know their opinion isn't going to change how I feel about you. Of course I want them to like you but if they don't," he shrugged, "their loss, not mine."

"But—" The doorbell cut off my retort.

Aidan went to the door while I listened. Soon the house was filled with a cacophony of exited voices and laughter.

"Jaysus, bro, you sure landed on your feet, didn't you? Huge improvement on that kip you used to call home."

I smiled and walked into the kitchen area, buying myself another minute or two before the inevitable introductions would have to be made.

"Lennart." Aidan's voice sounded much closer than I expected. "Come meet the mad ones." He squeezed my hand before allowing me to walk ahead of him into the living area. My heart thudded in my chest and I plastered a smile on my face as I prepared to meet the people who loved Aidan at least as much as I did.

"Mister Cassidy, Missus Cassidy." I held out my hand but Aidan's mother slapped it out of the way before wrapping me in hug.

"None of that nonsense, young man. I'm Bridget and himself," she pointed at the man who could only be Aidan's father, "is called Oliver."

My fake smile relaxed into a genuine one.

"The riffraff over there are Philomena, Rory and Connor, our baby."

"Ah, ma. Leave it off." The youngest Cassidy glared at his mother as a blush crept up his cheeks.

I fell in love with Aidan's mother there and then. She embodied everything I'd always imagined an Irish mammy to be, everything I'd never had in my life. All my worries evaporated as Aidan provided everyone with drinks.

"I want a beer too," Connor piped up again.

"Son, you're only seventeen." Oliver's voice was kind.

"But at home..."

"Does this look like our home?" Bridget turned to me. "If our host has no problem with it you can have one beer, but that's it."

I looked from one to the other. This family was like a verbal pinball machine with too many balls let loose at once.

"Why would I have a problem with it?" I had to think for a second before I remembered the lad's name. "If Connor having a beer is okay with you he's welcome to it." I glanced at Aidan, hoping I'd said the right thing. His warm smile reassured me.

Half an hour later I had a hard time remembering what exactly I had been worried about. His family were a pleasure to be around and if they didn't like me they had to be the most talented actors I'd ever met. We were about halfway through dinner when Aidan's father asked me about the house.

"Aidan told me some about how you got to live here. It's a rather sad story, lad."

I swallowed. The compassion in his voice touched something deep inside me.

"I'm sorry, but I have to say it as I see it," Bridget said. "Your father is a fool. There's nothing my kids could do that would make me turn against them." She semi-glared around the table. "And don't you lot take that as an invitation. Just because I wouldn't turn my back on any of yous doesn't mean I wouldn't give you shit for years to come if you gave me cause." The ensuing laughter broke what might otherwise have turned into a heavy conversation.

"Aidan says you write?" Philomena looked at me with curiosity in her eyes. When I nodded she continued. "What sort of stories? Would I like them?"

The blush crept up my cheeks as I turned to Aidan hoping he'd guide me through this minefield.

"Romances," Aidan answered the question for me. "Of the all-male variety."

Five pairs of eyes gazed at me as I did what I could to refrain from squirming.

"Cool." Aidan's sister smiled. "I'd love to read your stories when they're finished."

"Actually," Aidan waited to see if I would object before continuing, "Lennart is close to finishing his first book. I've read what he's written so far." He grinned. "I think it's good and," he winked at his mother, "rather hot."

"Good for you, young man."

I was surprised to receive the compliment from Oliver. If I'd been asked what the best case scenario would be, I'd have said I would be happy if nobody made fun of me or put me down for my writing. I'd definitely not expected this support from Aidan's father.

"I can't say I'm inclined to read it, but I've got a feeling Bridget will, and I applaud anyone who tries to turn their passion into a livelihood. I hope it works out for you."

By the time Aidan's family left again I not only felt as if I'd gotten away with it, I knew I'd been accepted. When Bridget pulled me to the side her words confirmed that impression.

"Thank you, love." She planted a firm kiss on my cheek.

"For what?"

"I haven't seen my son this happy and relaxed since before he left home. He refused to tell me what was wrong but I knew things were bothering him. He's been a different man these past few months, ever since he met you."

Her words made me glow inside but I had to put her straight. "You've got it all mixed up. Aidan's been the making of me, not the other way around."

She smiled at me. "That may be true too. But don't argue with a mother, lad. I know that boy." She directed a love-filled gaze at Aidan. "He's happy because he's with you. And that earns you a special place in my heart."

I cursed the tears burning in my eyes. If Bridget saw them she never let on.

Aidan and I watched as his family filed into their car. Aidan stood behind me and had his arms wrapped around my middle. As the car drove off he pulled me inside, closed the door and turned me around until I faced him.

"That was a good night, right?"

"The best." I grinned. "I love your family. They're mad, but I love them."

Aidan grinned back at me before pressing me up against the door and claiming my mouth for a long and hot kiss.

Chapter Eighteen

"Explain to me why you are the proud owner of a hurl. I thought you said you never played team sports." Aidan asked the question as we walked from the bus stop to the gates leading into the Phoenix Park. We were meeting Aidan's friends for a friendly game of hurling on what might well be the last nice day before the weather turned to wet and nasty.

"Oh, I played. I started when I was seven. I think it was part of my father's *man the boy* up plan." I could remember his words the first time he brought me to the local training grounds. *'Try not to disappoint me, Lennart. You need to be tough here. You can't burst out crying at the drop of a hat. Prove to me you're a man.'* At the time it had given me hope that if I just played the game well enough he might pay attention to me, love me even. "That was before I learned that things are never that easy."

I looked around at the vastness of the inner city park we'd just entered, reluctant to continue talking about my father. It wasn't my first time here. Aidan and I had been to the Zoo together during the summer and we'd cycled through the park a few times as well, taking advantage of Dublin City's rent-a-bike scheme. The sheer size of it still amazed me, as did the groups of deer wandering around.

"Were you any good?" Aidan's question drew my attention back to him.

"I used to think so. I mean, I almost always made the team when we had a match. I can't say I made any friends there but I wasn't bullied either. I was part of the team while we played. The rest of the time I was tolerated around the edges of their group." And I'd liked it. Hitting the slither, the rock hard little ball hurling was played with, as far and accurate as I could always satisfied a need in me. Every time I'd wacked the ball it had released some of the pent up aggression I harbored. And I'd felt safer with the hurl in my hand. Everybody had one of course but it made me feel as if I stood on an equal footing with the boys I played with. In fact, the hurling pitch was one of the few places I'd never encountered violence — other than the inevitable match play aggression of course.

"Why did you stop playing? Did you stop enjoying it?"

"I played until I was fourteen and I'm not quite sure what happened. My father pulled me from the club. He never gave me a reason, just said he didn't want to waste any more money on me."

"Did you mind?" Aidan asked.

"Yes. Yes, I did. I mean, it's not as if I had friends in the club or on the team, but I enjoyed playing and while nobody liked me, they did respect me for what I did in the matches." I stopped talking as memories I'd long since learned to repress, resurfaced. "It made things worse for me."

"How?"

"My old team lost the finals that year for the first time in three seasons, and people blamed me for it." I shrugged and tried to make light of it. "All it really meant was that my former team mates joined the army of my bullies."

"No offense but..." Aidan stopped talking and glanced at me.

"What?"

"Do you think your father wanted you to be alone and friendless?"

I stopped walking. Aidan's question shocked me to the core. Not because it didn't make sense but because it seemed to explain everything, except...

"Why would he do that? I mean it would explain his actions, but I don't understand what his reasons could be. I was his child. What did I ever do to deserve being treated like that?" I started walking again, suddenly too restless to stand still.

"I don't know." Aidan sighed. "But the more I hear of your past the less sense it makes. There has to be some explanation—no matter how twisted—even if we can't see it."

I allowed the idea to settle. Aidan's suggestion made more sense than any explanation I'd ever come up with, but still didn't provide me with any answers. I'd almost resigned myself to the fact I would probably never know exactly what had motivated my father.

"There they are." We'd rounded a corner and Aidan pointed to the center of a large field where ten of his friends and colleagues had already gathered.

"Better late than never." Larry's grin took the sting out of his words. He knew as well as we did that we weren't late at all. "Okay, now that the lover boys have arrived, let's team up."

A few weeks ago that description would have scared me, now it only made me smile sheepishly and blush. A few minutes later we'd split up into two teams of six, the goals had been marked and we were ready to play.

"A tennis ball?" I couldn't suppress my surprise.

"Well yes." Mark, one of Aidan's friends, smiled indulgently at me. "This is a public place. We have the field to ourselves now but for all we know it may be invaded by other people soon. If we accidentally hit someone with a slither..." He stopped talking and raised his eyebrow while I nodded. If I'd thought before I asked the question I would have realized playing with a real slither here was much too dangerous. There was a reason hurling players always wore helmets. Those slithers were lethal.

Ten minutes later, Larry slapped me on the back. "Jaysus, man, where'd you learn to play like that? I'm sure glad I picked you for my team."

I couldn't stop myself from grinning as I explained I'd played in the past.

"You should have stayed at it. You could have been good enough to make a county team." Larry walked on and rejoined the game as I stood and stared after him. Nobody had ever told me I was good at anything. Larry's remark had been completely off hand. He'd no way of knowing how momentous his words had been for me.

"What are you guys playing?"

I turned and faced the man with the American accent.

"I've never seen a hockey stick used like that before."

I glanced at the hurl in my hand and smiled. It wasn't dissimilar from a hockey stick, just as hurling wasn't a million miles removed from hockey. Except that it was a harder sport, played on a field rather than on ice and the players wore far less protection.

"It's called a hurl. It's an Irish thing. I don't think the sport is played anywhere else. In fact," I grinned at him, "I've seen hurling described as a cross between hockey and murder."

"I've never seen anything like it, that's for sure." The man smiled at me. "You looked impressive just now."

He winked at me and I blinked. Was he flirting with me?

"You okay?"

Aidan's arrival took me by surprise, but not nearly as much as him slipping his arm around my waist did.

Aidan and the American stared at each other for a moment while I tried to figure out what the hell was happening.

"Your boyfriend was explaining this game to me. I thought you guys were misusing hockey sticks." The American's words broke the tension and Aidan smiled. "Thanks for the explanation." The man nodded at me, and I imagined he looked a bit disappointed. "Have a nice day."

"I told you so."

I turned to Aidan. "What?"

"Didn't I tell you, you are cute?"

"Don't be stupid." I punched Aidan's shoulder but couldn't repress the tinge of pride his words awakened in me. "Come, let's play. I haven't beaten you by nearly enough goals yet." I grinned at Aidan before running off and throwing myself into the fray of the game again.

* * * *

"Have you thought about joining a hurling club in Dublin?"

I nearly spat out my mouth full of beer when Larry asked the question.

"Me? No..." I laughed. "The thought never crossed my mind."

"You should." He looked and sounded dead serious. "You're good. I'd love to have you on our team."

"Thanks." For the second time in a few hours, gratification flashed through me. "I'll think about it now." I looked across the table at Aidan and saw the pride in his face as he smiled at me.

I settled back in my seat and studied the people around me. I'd been out with these men before and they'd visited my house several times but I still couldn't believe how easily I'd slotted into their group. They'd taken me at face value. Right from the start my friendship — relationship — with Aidan had been enough for them. I'm sure initially they accepted me just because Aidan was their friend but now, three months later, I'd no doubt they liked me because of who I was. The experience was as wonderful as it was new.

Larry turned back to me and interrupted my happy reflections. "Now, explain to me how you managed to make the ball turn in the air like that."

I laughed and shook my head. My new life was a thing of wonder. I took in Larry's startled look before explaining in detail how he would need to twist his wrist when he hit the ball in order to achieve that curve.

Two hours later Aidan stared at me across the table in the restaurant where we'd stopped on our way home. He looked at me long enough to make me laugh nervously.

"What's wrong?"

"Absolutely nothing." Aidan grinned. "I can't believe you're the same person as the scared little boy I met three months ago."

"That's a good thing, right?" Just for a moment fear tried to wriggle its way into my consciousness before I shrugged it off. I had no reason to be afraid anymore – not with Aidan and not about Aidan.

"It's amazing." Aidan's face radiated happiness. "You've no idea how good it is to see you happy and unafraid."

"I couldn't have done it without you." I glanced at Aidan, suddenly shy.

"Rubbish. You would have got there with or without me." There wasn't a trace of doubt in Aidan's voice. "I may have sped the process up but all you ever needed was to get away from your old home. I just count myself lucky I get to reap the benefits."

I nearly laughed out loud. I knew I was the lucky one. I had no idea whether he was right or wrong in his assessment but I'd no doubt that even if I could have crawled out of the hole I'd buried myself in on my own, it would have taken me a lot longer. As far as I was concerned Aidan had been the making of me, and nothing he could say would convince me otherwise.

Chapter Nineteen

"Are you ready?"

I frowned at myself in the mirror. I looked ridiculous and couldn't believe I intended to go out dressed like this. Aidan had been messing with my hair until it fell any which way, with one or two tuffs sticking up to accentuate the disorganization. I scowled at the white shirt, gray jumper and yellow and burgundy tie.

"Hey, did you hear me?"

Aidan appeared behind me in the mirror and grinned. Trust him to look great. Dressed in identical outfits we should have looked the same. Yet here I was, a prime example of the ultimate dork, while Aidan, as always, looked hot as hell. The added dark rimmed glasses and the scar he'd painted on his forehead accentuated his cuteness and made me want to jump him there and then and forget about the evening ahead of us.

"I look like a bloody eejit. Why did I allow you to talk me into this?"

"You love me." His grin grew wicked and I couldn't help returning it.

"Yeah, I do. Sometimes I wonder if I don't love you too much."

"Come on. Stop moaning." Aidan punched me lightly. "It will be fun. What's not to like about a night out dressed up as Harry and Ron?"

"Going out as ourselves?" I raised an eyebrow at him before frowning at our costumes again.

"Stop sulking. We'll have fun. The whole town is going to be dressed up tonight. Besides, I can't go out with the lads from work and not wear a costume. Trust me, you got off light."

I nodded and smiled. Old habits apparently died hard but I was more than ready to embrace another new experience. I'd be a fool to spoil my first ever night out with the lads with my sulky behavior.

* * * *

At the restaurant, Larry, Aidan's manager, smiled at us when we reached the table. "Here we have Gryffindorians. Great outfits, lads, although it does remind me of this fan fiction my wife is forever talking about and reading. I'm not sure I want that image in my head right now."

My cheeks flamed up to match the color of my hair as some of Aidan's colleagues burst out laughing while others clearly had no idea what Larry meant. I did. I'd read some of those stories online and one quick glance at Aidan told me he had as well and that he'd had those very stories in mind when he'd suggested our costumes.

"Cockus Engorgio." Aidan smirked at me as he whispered the words while we sat down and damn if his words didn't have exactly that effect on me. I said a silent prayer of thanks for the tablecloth covering my crotch as I tried to ignore his still sniggering colleagues.

Twenty minutes and a pint later I had fully settled into the evening. Banter flew around the table and while I found myself the center of a slagging off on more than one occasion I couldn't claim they singled me out for it. As always, The Hidden Universe crowd pretty much indulged in equal opportunity teasing. Aidan had been right. Compared to his colleagues, our outfits were tame and boring. Five of them had teamed up to resemble The Avengers and to say not all of them were built to carry the costumes off would have been an understatement. I also had no idea why they'd decided the smallest of them had to be The Hulk. I didn't envy him having to go bare-chested this time of year and suddenly discovered a whole new level of appreciation for our shirts and jumpers.

Two hours later, Larry asked for and paid the bill.

"Okay, let's move this party on."

A seemingly endless queue of people waited outside the club Larry brought us to. Aidan and some others groaned when they realized we might have a long wait in the drizzly rain ahead of us but I didn't mind too much. If the line was anything to go by, the club would be packed. Just because I was no longer uncomfortable around people didn't necessarily mean I was comfortable in large crowds in confined places. I had no idea how I would fare. Going with a group of friends to a club aimed at the general public rather than the gay community, was another first for me.

Larry bypassed the line and walked straight to the bouncers. After a few minutes of friendly banter between Aidan's boss and the two men guarding the door our group walked in, earning us loud protests and quite a few angry stares from the people who'd been waiting for quite some time.

We fought our way through the sea of swaying bodies to a relatively quiet corner at the back of the club where Larry managed to grab a table and a few chairs. A few of the others went off hunting for more chairs while Aidan and I walked to the bar to get the first round of drinks.

"Enjoying yourself?" Aidan had to shout to be heard over the loud music and heavy bass.

"Yeah, I am." I was grateful the noise levels in the club meant Aidan couldn't hear the surprised note in my vote. I was enjoying myself a lot more than I'd thought possible before we went out. I ordered the round of drinks as soon as I captured a bartender's attention. While we waited for our order to be filled I glanced around the club and saw something that made me do a double take. *What the fuck?* I turned my head from left to right and back again, squinting my eyes in the harsh light. Had I really seen who I thought I'd recognized? Was I imagining things? I had to be hallucinating. No matter how hard I searched I couldn't detect the object of my fears again. My body tensed while my heart rate increased. I fought with myself. It didn't make sense for me to have really seen him. Somebody here resembled somebody I'd known at home. So what? No reason to panic and definitely no reason to spoil a fun night out.

"Are you okay? What's wrong?"

I cursed myself for my inability to hide my emotions and reactions from Aidan. Of course he'd picked up on my moments of discomfort.

"Nothing. I thought I saw someone I recognized but I must have been wrong." I smiled at him and breathed a sigh of relief when Aidan let it drop and turned to the bartender to accept our drinks.

I tried to forget what I thought I'd seen but couldn't stop myself from scanning the club while we walked back to the table holding a tray of drinks each. Five minutes and half a drink later I relaxed again and joined in with the shouted conversations around me.

"I wanna dance with you." Aidan's breath was hot against my ear as he shout-whispered the words.

I looked at the dance floor before nodding my head and getting up. The dance floor was a mass of swaying bodies. It was impossible to say who danced with whom and I felt sure we wouldn't stand out at all. A few of the Avengers joined us as Aidan and I moved to the middle of the club and joined the dancing mob.

Tonight was very different from the first time we'd danced together. Then it had been intimate, a form of seduction. Now we were just having fun with mates. I danced and laughed and didn't even flinch when Aidan snuck in a quick grope of my arse. Five songs later I felt as if I could keep this up forever when I saw them. I could feel the blood drain from my face as a cold sweat broke out all over my body. One of them stared hard at me while his mouth formed words I didn't need to hear in order to understand them.

"You're dead."

"Lennart. Talk to me. What's wrong?"

The worry in Aidan's face when I turned to him kick started my brain into overdrive. I had to get out of here, as soon as possible but I needed to go alone. No way would I pull Aidan into this nightmare with me.

"Sorry. I need to go." I looked around and the group of four I'd spotted only a moment ago had disappeared again but I no longer doubted what I'd seen. My past life had caught up with my present. Dublin wasn't any safer than the west coast had been.

Aidan grabbed my arm as I made to rise. "Tell me what's wrong. Then we go."

"No!" I plastered a smile on my face in the more than likely vain hope that Aidan wouldn't see through it. "You don't have to come with me. Stay. Have fun with your friends. I'll be fine." I knew he'd insist on coming with me if I told him what I'd seen and didn't want to take the risk.

"Don't be ridiculous. If you're going, I'm coming with you. Now please tell me what's wrong."

I hated his tenacity. I resented his ability to always spot when something bothered me and I wished I had it in me to ignore his demand and just get up and walk away.

"It's getting a bit too much for me." I waved my hand around. "Too many people, too much noise. I guess I'm not ready for a full night of it yet." I hated lying to Aidan but I couldn't think how else to stop him from coming with me. "Stay here. Enjoy the rest of the night with your friends. I'll be waiting for you in our bed. Say goodbye to Larry and the lads for me." I gave him the brightest smile I could muster before turning around and walking away, refusing him the opportunity to object. I knew he'd never leave the others without telling them first, which gave me all the time I needed to put some distance between us.

All my instincts screamed at me to run for the door and not stop running until I'd closed my front door behind me but I forced myself to slowly make my way to the exit. I heard him shout my name and, for the second time since I'd met Aidan, ignored it and kept on walking.

When I reached the street I walked only a few meters before I turned into an alley and pressed myself against the wall. My body shook and I didn't trust myself to go farther. I had to find some measure of control before I headed for home. Questions tumbled through my mind. I vividly remembered the expression on Gerard's face as he mouthed his threat. I'd recognized his grin. I'd seen it before whenever he and his mates had run into me somewhere they hadn't expected to find me. In the past they'd always taken advantage of the opportunity to hurt me. His words proved tonight wouldn't be any different unless I could stay away from them.

"Where'd he go?" It was impossible to not recognize the west coast accent. "He's not that far ahead of us. He has to be somewhere near."

I looked around, hoping to spot a place where I might hide but the alley held nothing except straight walls.

"Don't worry, we'll find him. He can't be far. How lucky were we?" The vehemence in Gerard's voice chilled my blood. "I thought it might take us days to find an opportunity to get to the little prick, only for him to present himself to us." His laughter increased my fear. "I guess some things are just meant to be."

I thought the subsequent silence was one of the scariest things I'd ever heard until Gerard spoke again. "Never mind. There's that faggot boyfriend of his. We'll get him. If nothing else, it will get the message across to the loser. "

Aidan.

All my instincts screamed at me to stay exactly where I was but my feet had a mind of their own. I reached the main street just in time to see Aidan being dragged into an alley farther down the road by Gerard and his mates. I ran to catch up with them before I could think about it. When I turned the corner, Aidan had been surrounded by them. One of them raised his hand to hit the man I loved.

"I think it's me you want."

"No! Run, Lennart. Go."

I ignored Aidan's words while willing the gang to switch their attention to me.

Gerard turned around and sneered at me. "Look, it's the little coward trying to act brave. Yes, we were looking for you, but this might work better. Maybe if we hurt your fuckbuddy enough you'll start paying attention."

I'd no idea what he meant nor the time to worry about it. I placed one foot in front of the other and moved closer to the group who'd returned their attention to Aidan.

"Let him have it, boys. We'll show these two just what we think of their kind, and deliver our message in the process." Gerard's voice sounded gleeful.

I started running the moment I saw them raise their hands. When the first blow landed on Aidan's head, I'd nearly closed the distance. I reached them in time to throw myself on top of Aidan after he'd fallen to the ground. I covered as much of his body with mine as I could while blows and kicks landed on my arms, legs, head and ribs. Pain shot from one location to another until it consumed me. I no longer knew where they hit me. The contact didn't register because every inch of my body already hurt. The pain, the continued attack and the damage they might be doing became irrelevant as I lay on top of an unmoving, silent Aidan.

A boot connected with the side of my head and blackness threatened around the edges of my vision.

"There they are. Hey, you lot. Leave them alone." Somewhere in the background I heard shouting and running footsteps but I couldn't concentrate. Words and partial sentences drifted through the fog as I tried to cling to consciousness, afraid they'd get to Aidan again if I didn't stay awake to protect him.

Lights flashed but I wasn't sure if they were real or the result of the kicks to my head. The clicking I heard sounded familiar but I didn't know what the noise meant.

"Did you get them? We won't get paid if you didn't."

"Yeah. I've got lots. Let's go."

The kicking stopped and running footsteps disappeared to one side as different feet approached from the other.

"Aidan, Lennart. Call nine-nine-nine." I recognized Larry's voice just before I let go and embraced the darkness.

Chapter Twenty

"How is he? Will he be all right?" The voice reached me through thick layers of fog. I knew I recognized it but couldn't pinpoint who it belonged to, before I drifted off again.

"…woken up yet. Should it take this long for him…?"

"No, I'm not going anywhere until I know…"

Fragments of sentences filtered through the fog. I thought about opening my eyes and finding out who the voice belonged to, but the dark blanket descended again.

"Lennart, wake up. Please, just open your eyes for a second. Please, love."

Aidan. Images flittered through my head. An alley, Aidan on the ground, me on top of him and pain.

The instant I remembered the pain I felt it too. Keeping my eyes shut I tried to locate where exactly I hurt and had to conclude my whole body had transformed into an agony filled vessel.

Something or somebody softly stroked my hair. "Please look at me, Lennart. Just for a moment."

Aidan. I tried to pry my eyelids apart. He sounded worried and upset and I wanted to reassure him. Harsh light made me close my eyes the moment I managed to open them, but not before I glimpsed Aidan next to me.

"That's it. You need to wake up now. You've been asleep for too long." The tenderness in his voice almost lured me back into oblivion but the slight slur I'd also noticed made me open my eyes again.

I stared at Aidan and the sight made me wish I'd kept my eyes closed. Half his face had swollen to twice its normal size and vivid colors spread from his neck to his hairline. I tried to lift my hand to touch him but my arm was too heavy.

"Don't move, love. You just needed to wake up. Nothing else."

"Thirsty." I could barely get the word past my dry lips. My mouth and tongue felt disfigured and out of practice.

"Here." He placed a straw between my lips. "Take it easy. Small sips. Don't make yourself sick."

I took a few sips and released the straw from my mouth, too exhausted to keep on drinking.

"The patient has woken up then?"

A new and unfamiliar voice kept me from falling back asleep.

"Okay, young man, let me have a look at you."

The woman pushing Aidan out of the way before bending over me wore a white coat and had a stethoscope around her neck. My sluggish brain took its time before it connected the dots and informed me I had to be in a hospital.

The doctor took a small penlight from her pocket and shone it in my eyes while moving it from left to right.

"Mmmmm."

"Is he okay?"

I turned my head to look at Aidan when I heard his voice and pain shot through my body.

"I told you, son, I can't give you any information. You're not family. I've only got your word for it you're his partner. You're lucky we've allowed you to stay here outside visiting hours as it is. Don't push your luck."

I moved my lips but no sounds escaped.

"What's that?" the doctor asked.

"Tell him." Even the soft whisper I managed to produce took huge effort. "He should know."

She looked at me and then at Aidan before answering me. "I'll tell you. If you want him to stay and listen there's nothing I can do about it. I can't break the confidentiality rules though. And, just something to think about, if you two want to avoid this sort of situation in the future, get something drawn up and signed by both of you." Her smile transformed her face and made her look less stern and exhausted.

"You, Mister Kenny…"

"Lennart, please. Mister Kenny is my father." A memory tried to surface as I mentioned my father but before I could pin the thought down it disappeared again.

"Well, Lennart, the short answer is that you're a mess but very lucky."

"And?"

"Most of your body is covered in bruises. Your ribs especially are going to hurt for weeks. But nothing is broken and I'm inclined to rule out concussion but we'll do a scan to confirm that. I'm sure it doesn't feel like it, but you should consider yourself fortunate."

I had trouble understanding her words. The way my body felt I'd been convinced at least half my bones were broken.

"In fact, just to check your stability I'd like you to get up and stand next to your bed within the next hour or so."

"You're joking." The words shot out of my mouth. I couldn't imagine getting up in the foreseeable future.

"No, I'm serious. And I can't let you go home until I have the scan results and know for sure you're not going to get sick once you're up and about."

I started to nod but stopped immediately as pain shot through my jaw. "What about Aidan?"

She sighed. "I can't tell you about him anymore than I could tell him about you. But, since he's up and about you can either draw your own conclusions or ask him?"

She turned around and walked away but stopped after a few steps. "A nurse will be with you to help you up in about an hour. I'll be back later today to discuss when you'll be released."

Aidan returned to my side before she'd left the room and I stared at his bruised face.

"How are you?" Guilt raged through me. If it hadn't been for me Aidan wouldn't be in this situation. I hadn't managed to convince him to stay in the club with his colleagues. He would have been safe there. I should have known he'd never let me go on my own. If only I'd dealt with the whole situation differently, Aidan's face wouldn't be the mess I saw in front of me now.

Aidan shrugged and I didn't miss the wince as it crossed his face. "I've been better, but it's not too bad. Compared to you it's nothing." He paused for a moment. "I'm so sorry Lennart."

The tears I heard in his voice shocked me. "You're sorry? Why are you apologizing? All of this is my fault."

"No. You don't get to claim this one." Aidan glared at me while simultaneously stroking his thumb over my hand. I should have never allowed you to walk away on your own. I knew there had to be a good reason, a reason you weren't telling me, for you to leave me there and go home alone. And still I took my sweet bloody time before following you." The moment I heard their voices, recognized their accents, I knew who they were, what you had done and why. You fool." His voice was soft and filled with regret. "Why didn't you tell me? I mean I'm right, aren't I? Those were lads from your old life back to torment you again, right?"

I nodded. "I didn't want them to hurt you. They were after me. There was no reason for you to get beaten up too."

"That's not how it works, Lennart." He smiled a sad smile. "We're in this together and that means all of it." He shook his head and grimaced. Anyway, it's not important. I managed to attract their attention and make them follow me and then…" His voice broke and with it my heart. "Then I wasn't strong enough to stay conscious and protect you. If it hadn't been for one of the lads having a smoke outside and seeing those thugs drag me into an alley, I don't know what would have happened to us."

"Aidan…"

"Larry told me what he saw when he caught up with us. You were lying on top of me taking all the kicks and blows. I'll never forgive myself."

I opened my mouth to tell him how wrong he was and closed it again. I knew none of what he'd said made sense but I had no idea how to convince him. The longer I stared at him and the tears he refused to let fall glistening in his eyes, the more certain I became I had to come up with something. I turned my hand and linked our fingers.

"If you hadn't met me, if we weren't living together, none of this would have happened to you. It only happened because you're with me. Don't you see?"

The two sentences had exhausted me and I closed my eyes for a moment.

"Lennart?" The hesitation in Aidan's voice tore at me. "Do you think it was a coincidence they were there?"

The moment he asked the question I remembered wondering the same thing when I'd first set eyes on them.

"I don't know." I sighed. "I want it to be a coincidence but it seems a bit much."

"That's what I thought."

We fell silent. I once again asked myself whether the encounter could have been a case of wrong place at the wrong time, and I assume Aidan pondered the same.

"By the way, the guards want to talk to you and take a statement."

"What?"

"Larry had to call an ambulance since we were both unconscious after those thugs ran from the scene. The police arrived at the same time. They've already taken my statement, for what it's worth, and will be back for yours."

Fuck. I didn't want to talk to them. The idea of telling them I'd recognized the lads and could name them scared the shit out of me.

"What did you tell them?"

Aidan looked at me as if I'd lost my mind. "What happened, of course. That I followed you when you left, was attacked by those men with west-coast accents and that you'd come to the rescue. I couldn't tell them a lot else. I can't remember anything after they hit me."

"Did you tell them you thought they were from my hometown?" I held my breath.

"Yes."

Despite the pain it caused I turned my head away and stared at the wall.

"What's wrong?"

"I don't want to name them." I turned back in time to see the surprise on Aidan's face and continued. "I'm scared. They're only four out of a much larger group. If I name them they may well end up in trouble but others will be back for revenge. Naming them will have the same result as painting a huge target on my chest and begging them to come and get me. If I let it be, ignore them, maybe they'll feel they've done enough damage and leave me —" I looked at him. "Us, alone."

"You can't do that. You can't let the bullies win. Oh shit, please don't cry."

The tears came as everything that had happened crashed in on me. The fear, the flight, the fight. All the confidence I'd gained over the past four months washed away as the tears ran down my cheeks.

"I'm sorry." I looked at Aidan, begging him to understand. "I can't do it. I'm going to tell them I don't remember, can't be sure anymore. Please don't be angry."

He stared at me for what felt like hours. I tried to read his face but emotions followed each other so fast I had to give up.

"I can't make you tell them anything you don't want to say. I think you're making a mistake, but if you can't do it…" His sentence tapered off and this time I could read his expression. He pulled himself together and plastered a well-meaning but clearly fake smile on his face.

"I guess we can always go back to them at a later date if you change your mind. You could always pretend the memory had only recently returned to you."

As he said the words I once again felt I'd forgotten something important, but I still couldn't put my finger on what it might be.

"Thank you."

Deep down inside I knew I'd made a mistake. Aidan was right. I shouldn't let the bullies win. Years of ignoring them hadn't stopped Gerard and his mates from harassing me. I just couldn't do it. Against my better judgment I still hoped the problem would disappear by itself. Involving the authorities would make my private problem public property. I clung to Aidan's words. I could backtrack at a later date. Maybe in a few days or weeks I'd find the courage to tell the guards all I knew.

Chapter Twenty-One

I stared at the words on my screen and hit the backspace key. The cursor flew backwards and took about ten seconds to get rid of the words I'd forced out over the past hour. Disgusted I pushed the chair away from my desk, got up and turned my back on my computer. Only a few more chapters and I'd have this book finished and I couldn't for the life of me get into the right mood to give my characters the happy ending they so richly deserved. In the kitchen I poured myself another cup of coffee and reached for the paracetamol before stopping myself.

I'd been home for a week. They'd released me the day after the attack. All in all I had been in hospital for about eighteen hours. The scan and all other test results had come back clean. While I'd felt like death on legs, there'd been no medical reason to keep me in. The first two days I'd been too weak and in too much pain to make it up the stairs so Aidan had dragged the mattress from the guest bedroom down and had made us a bed on the ground-floor.

I sipped my coffee while I walked back to my desk. Aidan had been great. He hadn't mentioned my refusal to name our attackers again, and I hadn't changed my mind. When the guard who came to take my statement asked, I told him I couldn't remember certain parts of the evening. I conceded it was possible I'd recognized the men but, added that I couldn't name them now. The officer had asked me a ton more questions—I assume in an effort to trigger my memories—but I'd stuck to my story and revealed nothing. Eventually he'd accepted that I couldn't provide him with the answers he needed and left, but not without instructing me to give a follow up statement if my memories returned.

I sat back down in my chair and put the coffee cup on the desk. I stared at the screen in front of me and the last line I'd written more than a week ago. Every time I'd tried to add to the story I'd ended up deleting all the words, just as I had today. My restlessness and inability to concentrate hadn't bothered me much while Aidan had been home. He'd gone back to work for the first time that morning and I felt lost on my own. Without my writing to distract from the long, lonely hours stretching ahead of me my mind went into overdrive.

I got up again, restless and impatient with myself. I didn't like the person I'd become after the attack. Or rather, the person I'd regressed to. I remembered myself like this all too well. Afraid to go out, bored at home and with no idea how to fix it. I almost resented the pain for fading. As long as every single movement had hurt me I'd had an excuse to linger in bed, to not go out—to spend my days in a lethargic heap on the couch. Not that the pain had disappeared, but as long as I didn't laugh or cry, refrained from making any sudden movements and didn't bend or stretch too enthusiastically, what had been severe pain remained a dull ache, a reminder of what had happened. Just as my reflection in the mirror still told a vivid and brightly colored tale of violence.

My phone made an incoming message sound and I grabbed for it so fast the ache in my ribs turned into a bright flash of pain.

How're you doing?

I loved Aidan for checking in on me and wished I could tell him something positive. I considered lying and rejected the thought. The relationship slope had become slippery enough without me making things worse.

OK. How about you? How's work?

It's fine, quiet. Wanna meet me for lunch?

My heartbeat increased and my stomach cramped when I read the question. I hadn't been out since coming home from the hospital and just the idea of leaving the house was enough to give me a panic attack. I took too long answering, and his next message appeared on my screen.

Never mind. Maybe I'll take you for a pint in the local tonight. You can't stay cooped up inside forever.

Why not? I didn't type the words because even I knew how ridiculous they sounded but if anybody had offered me the opportunity to spend the rest of my life indoors I'd have taken it without a second thought.

Yeah. Maybe.

I didn't want to leave the safety of our house. Not even to our local although I had grown to love that pub over the past few months. I wouldn't worry about it until Aidan came home though.

What are you doing? Writing?

I glanced at the screen on my desk and grimaced.

No. The words won't come. I think I'll have a look at those notebooks of my grandda's.

I had no idea where the idea came from but it perked me up instantly. I'd been postponing my further investigation of that box for reasons I couldn't even explain to myself. Today I needed to feel less alone. Maybe spending some time with my grandfather, even if he had died, would make me less despondent.

Great idea. Can't wait to hear what you find.

He didn't say it, but then, he didn't need to. I could read his relief that at last I'd decided to do something, underneath the words on the screen.

Gotta go back to work. C U L8er.

I kept my return text short and to the point.

<3

I felt revived by my idea and didn't waste any time. Pulling out the box hurt me more than I liked but for the first time in a week I ignored the pain and just continued what I'd started. I picked up the first notebook I saw and opened it. The date showed me the entries had been written in nineteen ninety-seven, when I had been three and it had been over two years since the one and only time my grandfather and I had been in each other's presence as far as I knew.

I flicked through the book and got glimpses of another happy gay couple living in this house. The entries were mundane and mostly short. Day trips, special dinners, funny moments. With every page I felt closer to the man I'd never known.

My grandfather had been a regular writer and it made me smile. I liked the idea our sexual orientation wasn't the only thing we had in common. When I came to a two month long gap between entries my curiosity peaked. Five minutes later I wished I'd picked up one of the other books.

June 10, 1997
It's been a long time since I last wrote and I've missed it. Writing with a broken hand is impossible though so I had to wait. Putting pen to paper still hurts but now that the whole affair is behind us, if not resolved, I want to write it down and try to forget about it.

It happened on the eighteenth of April. I'd booked a table in Monty's of Kathmandu so Sean and I could celebrate Lennart's birthday with a nice dinner.

I nearly stopped reading there. Tears burned in my eyes at yet another confirmation that my grandfather had loved and missed me. I knew without any doubt I didn't want to read the rest of the entry but couldn't make myself put the notebook away.

God I miss that boy. I'll never forgive Thomas for keeping me away from him.
Anyway, the dinner was wonderful and Sean as supportive as he always is. I've no doubt it gets frustrating for him to

listen to me moan about the grandchild I've lost and I'm all too aware I make him sad and insecure every time I mention it.

It was a lovely evening, especially for April so we decided to walk home. As soon as we turned the corner from the restaurant, we were confronted by three men. I'd never seen them before and don't think I'd recognize them if I met them again but I did recognize the west coast accents.

They jumped on us before we realized we'd run into trouble. By the time they'd finished hitting and kicking us I knew my hand was broken and Sean was on the ground, barely conscious. I thought we had the worst of it behind us when those men walked away, laughing at us and shouting that they hoped we'd learned our lesson.

The real nightmare started after we'd been treated in the hospital and had to talk to the gardai. I knew it wouldn't go well the moment he looked at us. I'm not going to write the details down although I can remember that encounter word for word. Suffice to say he made it clear he'd take down the details because he had to but thought we'd only ourselves to blame for what had happened. I don't expect an investigation ever to take place and it infuriates me.

I try to remind myself it's only been four years since homosexuality was decriminalized but it doesn't help. Finding myself on the receiving end of a beating was bad enough. Discovering the law doesn't give a shit what happens to me makes me want to scream.

When a tear smudged words on the page in my hands—adding to the smudges already there—I pushed the notebook away. I didn't know what to make of what I'd just read. The parallels were too extreme. The likelihood of both him and me finding ourselves on the receiving end of west coast fists had to be slim to none and yet it had happened. I felt guilty it had happened because they'd gone out to celebrate my birthday fully aware how unreasonable the thought was.

West coast accents. The words spun through my head while my mind jumped to a conclusion I didn't want to examine. No matter how big a bastard I knew my father to be, I didn't want to believe he'd set two relatives up for beatings. And yet, the similarities were too striking for it to be a coincidence. If his attackers had been Dublin natives or from the North or anywhere but the West, I wouldn't have thought about it twice.

No. I forced the idea away. Coincidences did happen. Nearly fifteen years separated the two attacks after all.

I stared at my laptop as a fully formed plot for my next book revealed itself to me. I might not have it in me to finish the rather light and goofy story in my first novel right now, but I knew exactly what to do with the next one. It would be dark, very dark, but I needed to write it. For my grandfather, for Aidan and for me.

* * * *

"Why are there no lights on here?"

Aidan's voice pulled me out of my trance.

"You're home? What time is it?" I blinked as Aidan hit the light switch and the room sprang to life around me.

"Half-past six. Same time I always come home." Aidan walked farther into the room and put his hands on my shoulder when he arrived behind me. "You've reacquainted yourself with your muse then?"

"Hmmmm." I stared at the screen and checked the word count.

"Holy shit. You wrote all of this after we texted?" Apparently Aidan saw the same thing I did. Over five thousand words in four hours, it was a personal record by a large margin.

"Yes. I guess I did."

"No wonder you forgot the lights. This is something different though."

I looked at him before getting up and retrieving my grandfather's journal. The shifting expressions on his face as he read the entry reflected all the emotions I had felt earlier.

"Holy fuck. Your grandda and you are alike in ways that make me uncomfortable."

I nodded.

"You know what? I want to talk about this." He pointed at the notebook. "And about what you're writing, but right now I'm starving."

"Shit. I'm sorry." I felt terrible. We'd never talked about it and I knew he didn't expect it from me but we'd grown into a routine where I'd have dinner ready or at least cooking by the time he came home from work.

"Don't worry about it. As far as I can see, you spent the time well. Besides, I wanted to take you to the pub anyway. We might as well grab a bite to eat there."

My stomach knotted up the moment he said the word pub.

"Yeah, about that…"

He didn't say a word, just looked at me with that gaze of his, the one that told me to stop being a fool.

"Okay. Yeah." I took a deep breath. I could do this for him, I had to. "Right—if we're gonna do this, we'd better do it now, before I lose my nerve."

* * * *

"Well, strangers, I thought we'd lost you for good." Noel behind the bar grinned at us as we walked in and some of the tension left me again. Our local had been a safe and friendly place from the first time we walked in together.

When we got closer to the bar he looked at us and a frown appeared on his face. "I'm not gonna ask since it's none of my business but I see why you haven't been out for a while. Here," he pulled two pints and put them on the bar, "on the house."

"Thanks," we replied at the same time before Aidan continued. "We'd like a bite to eat, what's the special?"

As soon as we'd ordered our fish and chips we sat down at a small table.

"You okay?" Aidan closely inspected my face, looking for signs of discomfort.

"Yes, I'm fine." I looked around the pub I'd grown quite fond of over the past few months. "I'm sorry I gave you a hard time about coming here. I should have known it would be fine."

Aidan shrugged. "You weren't ready before tonight. Now you are. Nothing to apologize for." He thought for a moment. "About your grandda…"

I nodded although I didn't want to go where I thought he was about to take the conversation.

"It's a bizarre coincidence don't you think?"

"My grandfather and his partner getting beaten up?" I'm not sure why I asked the question.

"That, and by men with West Coast accents." Aidan frowned.

"Yeah. But it has to be a coincidence, surely. I mean there's fifteen years between the two events." Tension started to build in my stomach again and when the food arrived I stared at it, my appetite gone.

"I don't know, a coincidence is one thing, this on the other hand takes the concept a bit far, don't you think? And I don't suppose we'll ever figure it out one way or another." He sighed. "Tell me what you've been writing about."

Although the new story I'd started had been inspired by the two attacks I didn't mind talking about it. I relaxed as I spoke and before I knew it we'd both finished our dinners, as well as two pints each and I'd outlined the whole story I had in mind to Aidan.

"Well," Aidan leaned back in his chair, "that's a complete departure from the story you've nearly finished."

He had a point, but strange as it felt, even that evening I knew that writing the dark story would enable me to finish the lighter one. I had to find a way of dealing with everything that had happened, and all the discoveries I'd made. Writing had always allowed me to make sense of my life and I had every confidence it would do so again.

The pub got busier around us and while I didn't feel panicky I did grow restless and couldn't stop myself from looking around and checking the faces of everybody who entered.

"I think that's enough for your first night." Aidan's smile was radiant. "You lasted longer than I thought you would. Let's go home and have a private party." He wiggled his eyebrows and smirked before leaning toward me and whispering in my ear. "I've got plans for you."

I blushed and couldn't stop myself from looking around to make sure nobody had heard him or taken offense to our closeness. Reassured, I turned back to him. "Gonna tell me what those plans are?"

"You'll see." Aidan's dirty grin heated my blood.

We walked home and when he took my hand in his I didn't worry. I knew I still had a long way to go before I'd get even a semblance of confidence back but I'd taken the first, tentative, steps.

Chapter Twenty-Two

"Listen, I've changed my mind. Let's go home."

"No, we're going dancing to celebrate." Aidan didn't even slow down while I dragged my feet in an effort to postpone our imminent arrival at the place I didn't want to visit.

"How is it a celebration if I don't want to do it?" *God.* I hated myself when I sounded like a spoiled five year old.

"You want to dance with me. You know you do." Aidan's lopsided grin, combined with a lazy wink, elicited a small smile from me.

"I always want to dance with you, but we could have danced at home."

Aidan stopped walking and looked at me. "Yes, I know we could have. That's what we've been doing for the past month. Our whole lives, or rather your whole life, has taken place within those walls. It's time to break them down again."

He grabbed my hand and started walking again, leaving me no choice but to follow in his footsteps. I still wasn't sure how he'd managed to talk me into this.

I'd wanted to tell him the moment he walked through the door but waited until he'd showered and we were having our dinner.

"So. I did it."

"Hmmm?" Aidan had clearly been miles away.

"I did it. I submitted my book today." I felt my face change expression every other second, stupid grins and nervous smiles replacing each other in rapid succession.

I'd spent most of the day staring at the email I'd written. The story and synopsis had been attached and all that remained was for me to press send. Who knew one click with a mouse could be so hard? I'd walked away from the computer several times and had cleaned the house just to give myself something to do.

As soon as I made my announcement Aidan had stopped eating and turned to me.

"That's great. Oh, man. I'm so proud of you."

"Thanks," I answered as soon as he'd stopped kissing me. "It's one of the scariest things I've ever done."

"Don't worry about it. You wrote a good story. I have no doubt they'll accept it. No doubt what so ever."

"Yeah, right." I laughed. "You have to say that. You're my boyfriend."

I'd expected him to laugh along with me but found myself looking at a thoughtful and serious expression on his face instead.

"Why do you do that?"

"Do what?" The nervous laugh accompanying my words didn't sound anything like the earlier one.

"Put yourself down like that? You know the story is good."

I sighed. I knew no such thing but I did know he thought the story was good. He'd read and corrected it for me once I'd finished the first draft and he'd not gone easy on me. He'd questioned and pushed me until I wanted to scream at him. Every time he suggested a change it had frustrated me. But he'd been right more often than not. The story I'd submitted was a lot better than it had been before he got his hands on it.

"Maybe," I answered. "That didn't stop me from wanting to change at least five things as soon as I sent it on its way."

"Do you know how long it will take until you hear back from them?"

"I've no idea. According to the website it can take up to eight weeks so I won't be holding my breath." But I had no doubt I would be stalking my inbox while I pretended not to be waiting.

Every step we took brought us closer to the destination I didn't want to reach. The Friday night crowds were loud and boisterous and the fog hanging over the city did nothing to lessen my apprehension.

"Will you walk? If you slow down anymore we'll be going backwards."

I had to admire Aidan's patience. He'd been trying to talk me into going out for the past two weeks and I'd been stalling. Until tonight. When Aidan suggested we'd visit the club where we'd first met to celebrate, I hadn't been able to bring myself to kill his enthusiasm. He'd been more than patient with me while I fell back into my old habits of hiding from the world and I didn't want to be that person again. Neither his enthusiasm nor my desire to be more relaxed and outgoing, were strong enough to stave off the rising panic inside me.

Two minutes later I found myself on the sidewalk opposite the entrance to the club again. Five months ago, I'd stood here with my back pressed against the wall while I worked up the courage to cross the street and enter unchartered territory. This time we didn't stop.

Just like the first time I came here the club was still relatively empty. We got our drinks from the bar and went straight to the seating area, opting to sit on a couch together rather than in two separate chairs. Aidan put his hand on my leg and gave me one of his winning smiles.

"See, that wasn't so hard."

"So far so good." I admitted despite the solid lump of panic sitting in my stomach, waiting to erupt. "I'm not sure how I'll manage when it gets busier."

"Don't worry about it. We'll play it by ear. As long as I get at least one dance with you out of tonight I don't mind when we go home again." I felt his hand on my thigh, his fingers drawing circles close to my crotch, and had to remind myself it was perfectly acceptable behavior in this club.

"Relax, Lennart. Stop looking around, nobody is about to bother us here." His voice got lower. "Just concentrate on my hand."

I laughed. "Your hand's what has me worried."

"Why? Are you afraid it might do this?" He fondled my cock and balls and I almost whimpered.

"Aidan, please."

"Please what? Please more? Please stop? Tell me." I didn't understand the urgency I heard in his voice.

"Please... I don't know."

He frowned for a moment before leaning over and giving me a soft, quick, kiss. "Don't think about it too much. Concentrate on enjoying yourself, us. We're safe here, I promise."

His hand continued to tease my thigh and crotch and despite my anxiety, or maybe because of it, I could feel heat gathering in my loins. My mind might have been running in scared circles, my body had no doubt it enjoyed the attention it received.

We talked as the club filled up and watched people, while we indulged ourselves in gossip and speculation about those around us. Gradually my mind slowed down and my body relaxed. As the dance floor got busier I couldn't stop my leg from bouncing to the rhythm assaulting our ears, and when Aidan stood and pulled me up I didn't think twice before following him and surrendering to the beat.

My thoughts and fears disappeared as I lost myself in the sea of moving bodies, all in the grip of the same, almost hypnotic, cadence. I couldn't keep my eyes off Aidan. He danced as if he'd been born for that purpose. His body moved with ease and exuded raw sex. When, after we'd been dancing for I don't know how long, he pulled me close and ground our bodies together, I allowed it to happen without hesitation.

I lost myself in the sensations his closeness awoke in me. For the first time since our disastrous night out I felt free. My cock had grown pleasantly hard and I loved feeling his arousal against mine. I closed my eyes and allowed myself to just feel the beat, Aidan and this rediscovered sense of freedom. The feeling evaporated as someone pushed up against my back. Even without being able to see who it was or why it happened I knew it couldn't be an accident. A cock ground into my arse and pushed me closer to Aidan. I opened my eyes as my body tensed.

"Relax. It's just a bit of fun." Aidan kept his voice soft and soothing. It did little to dispel the panic growing inside me. Aidan wrapped an arm around me and pulled me closer. "It's a compliment." He murmured the words into my ear. "He's showing you how sexy you are when you dance. Don't look but he's cute."

As much as I didn't want them to, Aidan's words excited me. Heat battled with panic and I didn't know whether I wanted it to stop or continue indefinitely.

"I bet he wants you. I can see it in his eyes. He's hot for you."

The belligerent voice in my head told me Aidan was wrong. I wasn't sexy. Just because Aidan couldn't see, or refused to accept how ordinary and needy I was didn't mean others found me attractive. The hard cock's continued presence against my backside told a different story.

When I felt an arm snake around my middle from behind I stiffened again, the only thought in my mind to run as fast and as far as I could. I stared at Aidan's face and saw him look past me and shake his head. The arm disappeared again and, as one song changed into another, so did the presence behind me.

My mind reeled. What had just happened? What did it mean?

"Don't over think it, Lennart." Aidan stared at me. "Wanna go home now? It's been fun but it's getting too packed here, even for my liking."

I just nodded my head, too lost in my thoughts to speak. When he flagged down a taxi as we came out of the club I breathed a sigh of relief but still didn't talk. I didn't say a word on the way home either and barely heard the taxi driver grumbling about us living so close by, the trip hadn't been worth his while.

I entered our house as if in a trance and automatically walked up the stairs to our bedroom. I stripped, brushed my teeth and crawled into the bed. For the first time since Aidan had moved in I wouldn't have minded an hour or so by myself. My thoughts tumbled through my head too fast for me to keep track of them. I hated to admit it but I'd enjoyed that person grinding up behind me once I'd let go of the initial panic. I thought that should mean something but couldn't for the life of me figure out what exactly.

"Lennart?"

"Yeah." I gazed at the man lying next to me in bed and tried to figure when he'd arrived there. I hadn't been aware of him when I walked up the stairs, hadn't seen him undress and hadn't noticed when he got into the bed.

"I didn't go too far, did I?"

"What do you mean?" I couldn't make sense of his words. In fact I couldn't make sense of anything.

"In the club, the groping, the dancing, me allowing that man to grind up to you, it was okay, wasn't it?"

I'd been asking myself the same questions. Not whether or not Aidan's actions had been okay but what to make of my reactions to them. For both our sakes I had to come up with an answer.

"Honestly?"

He nodded.

"Well, at first it wasn't." A shadow crept over his face and he opened his mouth to say something. I pressed my middle finger to his lips and continued. "It made me nervous and even more self-conscious than I normally am. I kept on checking to see if people were looking at us. But nobody was."

I grinned and Aidan's worried expression relaxed some. "In fact, most of those who weren't paying attention to us were far too busy with similar explorations of their own partners. When I felt that body behind me I thought my heart might stop beating."

Aidan tensed up again and for the second time I thought he would interrupt me, so I hurried along with my next words. "And then, later, it was okay."

I recognized the incomprehension in his eyes and continued, grateful that his question forced me to work this out for both of us.

"It took time but I relaxed and enjoyed it. I'm sure the drinks we had before we danced helped, and I've no doubt I would have panicked if you hadn't held me close, but yeah…" I smirked, "Surely you noticed how much I enjoyed it." I lowered my hand and stroked my semi-hard cock.

His eyes darkened as he watched me coaxing my dick to full attention. "Welcome back." All tension had disappeared from his face and body as he moved closer and kissed me. "You're so sexy when you're confident and happy."

I stared at him and for a moment I allowed the rage to consume me. He'd pushed me to my limit on purpose. The risk he'd been willing to take took my breath away. If he'd pushed too hard, if I had panicked, if anybody in that club had looked at us askance it might have broken me, broken us. My breath faltered as I recognized the magnitude of what he'd done.

"Jaysus, Aidan. What a risk to take." My anger faded.

His voice was soft and he didn't look at me. "I had to. I couldn't do it anymore. I'd seen you change from someone afraid of his own shadow into somebody who knows what he wants and goes for it." His voice got louder. "And those bastards took it all away. The longer you were stuck in the house the more you seemed to shrink. It was as if you were fading before my eyes. I had to get you back." He turned his head and his eyes were filled with love and something suspiciously like tears. "I didn't know how else to do it."

I allowed his words to hang in the air between us while I tried to figure out how I felt about what he'd said, what he'd done, his huge gamble. Our crotches were pressed together, my still hard cock pressing into his semi. He'd taken a chance because he wanted to help me back from the threshold. I considered asking him whether he'd had all of it planned. Had Aidan organized the man grinding up to me beforehand or had his actions been as a big surprise and shock for Aidan, as they had been to me? The question almost left my lips before I realized it didn't matter. He'd decided to force me out of my shell, to make me face the world and live again and he'd succeeded. It had been difficult and I'd had one or two anxious moments but thanks to the unimaginable risk he'd been willing to take with me, with himself, with us, I once again believed life could be more than surviving in seclusion.

I didn't know how to verbalize everything I thought and felt so I did the only thing I could think of in response to the evening we'd just had. I wrapped my hand around both our cocks and without taking my eyes off him for a single moment slowly stroked both of us to an orgasm that felt, for me at least, as if it came from my toes.

Chapter Twenty-Three

December, 2013

I'm sorry it had to come to this. You may not believe me but I never wanted this affair to deteriorate the way it has and will continue to do, unless you decide to come to your senses. You know me well enough to realize I always get what I want. That house you live in should be mine. Just because the law allows parents to disinherit their own children doesn't make it right and I intend to make sure I get what I'm entitled to.

I've tried to get this message across to you in various ways, all of which you've decided to oppose or ignore. I'm asking you one last time to do the sensible thing and sign my property over to me now. I need a house in Dublin if my plans are going to come to fruition, and the property on Adelaide Road would be perfect.

If you continue to ignore me, I'll have to take further measures and I've reached the stage where the gloves are off. I'd prefer it if we could just go our separate ways and forget about each other, but I will have what should be mine to begin with first, no matter what the price. Neither you nor your fuckbuddy is safe until I have what I want.

I got up as soon as I read the last word. The letter slipped from my fingers as I ran to the bathroom. With my head over the toilet bowl, I got rid of the nausea the vile words had induced. The address on the envelope had been typed, as was the unsigned letter itself. Even without a signature I'd no doubt who'd written the threatening words. I also remembered what I'd forgotten. I remembered their words. *'Did you get them? We won't get paid if you didn't'* and *'Yeah. I've got lots. Let's go.'*

With the words came the memory of the clicking sounds I'd heard and the flashes I'd seen, even with my eyes closed and barely conscious. The men who'd beaten us up had taken pictures because they'd needed proof. I could imagine the scenario. My father had always thought everything could be got provided you paid enough. He must have offered them money — or something else they needed — in return for beating the shit out of me. And he wasn't done.

I didn't have the strength to get up. Despite the stink of the vomit I rested my head on the arms I clung to the bowl with, and closed my eyes. My father would get this house, no matter what he had to do to achieve his goal. His vendetta against me had lost all pretense of having anything to do with justice. This was a quest, my father's way of punishing both me and my grandfather for being who we were. For loving in a way he found disgusting.

I knew I had decisions to make. I couldn't expect Aidan to stay with me and face this. My heart broke as I came to what felt like the only possible conclusion. When Aidan came home tonight I'd have to tell him he needed to leave. The only issue I hadn't figured out yet was how much to tell him. I knew him well enough to know he'd never leave if I told him the truth. I had about four hours to come up with a convincing reason why I needed him out of my house and life.

I pushed up, flushed the toilet and poured some cleaner in, before dragging myself to the bedroom. Overcome by a sudden exhaustion, I collapsed on top of the bed. The idea of having to lie to Aidan, of trying to convince him I didn't want him in my life and house anymore, brought tears to my eyes. I needed to rest and attempt to quiet my mind before facing the toughest thing I'd ever done in my life.

* * * *

"Lennart."

The soft voice forced me to return from the darkness I'd fled to.

"Wake up, baby."

I felt fingers in my hair, stroking my head. I sighed and relaxed into a feeling of deep contentment. I kept my eyes closed and the world at bay for as long as I could. Something tugged on the edges of my memory and I knew I'd lose this comfort as soon as I recalled what it was.

"I can tell you're awake, you know." The deep rumble of Aidan's voice and his Dublin accent touched places in me I'd never known could be affected by anyone. I turned on my back and opened my eyes to see the man I loved sitting on the side of my bed. He still had his fingers in my hair and used them to massage my scalp. From the corner of my eye I saw the piece of paper he held in his other hand and my heart stopped.

"You found it?" Inside my head a voice screamed at me. How could I have been so stupid? Why hadn't I picked the bloody letter up before going to bed?

"Well yes. It was hard to miss, seeing how it lay on the floor in the middle of the hall."

I hadn't even thought about the letter after I got sick, never mind noticed that I'd dropped it along the way. And now Aidan knew.

"Did you call the guards?" He continued caressing my head.

"What? No."

"Why the hell not? Even if he didn't sign the letter, it's clear your father wrote it. He all but admits he organized the beating. You've got to report him or he'll never stop."

To Aidan it all appeared straightforward. I got that. I would have felt the same if our positions had been reversed. But he didn't know my da. He'd no idea what I was up against or what might happen if I didn't comply.

"Because I'm afraid it might make things worse. My father is friends with everybody who is anybody in our town, including the guards. At best they'd tell him to be less obvious about it in future."

The disbelief on Aidan's face was clear. "I refuse to believe that. Even in rural Ireland things can't be that bad. Besides, you wouldn't be reporting to those local guards. We'd be talking to officers here, the same ones who interviewed you in hospital." His expression changed as something occurred to him. I knew what he'd say next. I had known it would come back to haunt me when I made my statement and now the moment had arrived.

"You never went back to tell the guards you knew who they were did you?"

I tried to turn my head away but the fingers that had been giving me a wonderful head massage now firmly held me in place. "No, I didn't."

"Lennart, man, what's wrong with you?"

"I knew. Even then I suspected why they attacked us. I never for one moment thought my former bullies would have taken the train to Dublin just to hurt me. They never hated me that much. In fact, I never aroused much of any sort of emotion in them. I used to be an easy victim, so they targeted me. I knew they had to have an added incentive to do what they did." I stopped talking. It would upset Aidan enough that I'd kept all of that to myself. He didn't need to know the rest.

"There's more. What else did you forget to tell me and the guards?"

I almost smiled at this proof of how well he'd gotten to know me over the past few months. Under any other circumstances I would have been delighted he saw right through me.

"I really had forgotten about this. I only remembered after I read the letter but..." I hesitated before continuing. "I heard them talk. Just before I passed out they told each other to make sure they got the pictures or they wouldn't get paid."

"Jaysus, Lennart. Did you have any intention of telling me that? Of reporting it?" Aidan got up and walked to the window. The tension in his back screamed his frustration.

"I'm not sure."

I watched him in silence. Any words I might say, any excuse I tried to come up with wouldn't change the fact I'd been willing to keep these things from him. Time went by and every minute of silence seemed to add another brick to the wall rising between us. A wall I'd laid the foundations for in the attack's aftermath.

My heart broke when Aidan turned back and faced me. His eyes were bright with unshed tears. "I thought you trusted me."

"I do. I really do." I thought about my next words. I had to get them right. He would have to leave me. After the letter we both knew how dangerous it would be for him to stay here. But I needed him to know he had to leave because I loved him and not for any other reason.

"I was scared, I still am. You don't know my father. You have no idea about the sort of influence he has. I've been trying to figure out whether I should just hand the house over to him or stay and see how far he will go. I mean if he kills me he'll get punished, won't he? Even his friends won't be able to help him then."

The pain in my chest felt real. I'd never suspected a broken heart was more than just a metaphor.

"You see, even if I do what you want and go to the guards..."

"There's no bloody if about it." Aidan was livid. "You're going to the guards first thing tomorrow if I have to drag you there kicking and screaming. This is going to end now."

"You don't understand." I hated the pleading note in my voice. "Best case scenario, right? I take the letter and my memories and report them and the guards take my word for it and investigate my claims. It's not as if my father would be arrested immediately. Even if it comes to a prosecution, he'll be a free man until he's convicted. I know him. He's not going to sit back and wait to see what might happen. He'll act and he'll want to hurt me as much as possible. Just the house won't be enough anymore. He'll go after you."

I saw the images as I spoke the words. The memory of Aidan's battered and bruised body fresh enough for me to have no problem imagining what he would look like after another beating, or even dead.

He walked back to the bed and sat down next to me again. I only realized I'd started crying when he stroked the tears off my cheek with his thumb. "Don't you see? No matter what I do next, it's too dangerous for you to stay with me. I can't ask you to do that. I couldn't cope with you being hurt again, just because you're my boyfriend."

His kiss was soft and soothed me. I wanted to crawl into his lap. I wished I could just lock the doors and keep the world outside, make my father and the problems he caused go away. I'd never been happier than I'd been during the past few months. Loving Aidan and being loved by him had changed my life, and me. Having to give it up broke my heart.

"You need to go, Aidan. If you're no longer living with me in this house, you'll be safe from him and whatever he might decide to do in the future" My voice broke on the words.

"No." His voice was calm.

"Aidan, listen…"

"No."

"But…"

"No." I heard no doubt, anger or confusion in his voice. I'd never seen him as determined. "I'm not leaving you. Imagine what it would be like for me if I went. I'd spend every minute of every day worrying about you, wondering whether your father would send somebody after you again, afraid you'd get yourself hurt." He sighed. "It's not that I don't understand why you want me gone. I understand it all too well. The reasons you want me to go are the same as my reasons for staying. Don't fight me on this. I'm not going regardless of what you do or say."

Relief and despair battled for dominance inside me. Even imagining what living without Aidan would be like had been painful, but I didn't know how to deal with the fact that the danger he faced resulted directly from his relationship with me.

"If something else happens to you, I'll never forgive myself."

"I know," Aidan said. "I feel exactly the same about you. That's why we have to stick together. We can deal with this. We'll go to the guards tomorrow and hand all we have over to them. If nothing else, having to face an investigation will force your father to think twice before he tries something else."

Aidan's argument didn't convince me. He didn't know my father. I did, and I knew nothing made him more unpredictable than being forced into a corner. But I had no doubt Aidan had made up his mind. Short of ending our relationship, I had no hope of making him leave me.

I actually thought about it. I tried to imagine telling him I didn't want him in my life or my house anymore and came up empty. Even if I could make myself say those words I wouldn't be able to make him believe I meant them. I cursed my selfishness. His safety should be more important than my need to be with him. If I loved him enough I'd be able to send him away.

"Lie down." Aidan climbed on the bed and stretched out next to me. We faced each other and he pulled me close. "I know you, Lennart. You are trying to convince yourself sending me away would be the loving thing to do, aren't you?"

There were moments I hated his uncanny ability to read my mind.

"You'd do it." I still wasn't ready to give up the fight. "If you thought being away from you would be best for me you'd send me away." I stared at Aidan, daring him to deny it.

"Probably." He smiled. "But would you go?"

He had me. I wouldn't be able to leave no matter what the circumstances. My inability to leave him when he faced trouble or violence had become only too clear when he'd been in danger.

Anger born from frustration made me push him on his back and climb on top of him.

"I hate it when you're right." I cringed when I recognized how childish I sounded. Aidan just laughed.

I looked at the man beneath me, his messy hair, the last remnants of a tan, and the big dark eyes that shone with heat and amusement as he returned my gaze. I loved this exasperating man so much it scared me.

I bent forward, took his bottom lip between my teeth and pulled not altogether gently. He raised his eyebrow and groaned at the same time. We'd entered new and uncharted territory. I'd never taken control like this before.

I nibbled on his lip before releasing it and stroking it with my tongue. "You infuriate me." I murmured the words, most of my frustration having disappeared again. "You're stubborn. You make me do things I don't want to do. And you're almost always right. Remind me why I put up with you?"

His lips had parted and he flicked his tongue over the spot I'd bitten and licked. "You love me."

The tenderness in his voice nearly floored me. I bent forward again and took possession of his mouth. I put everything in that kiss, the depth of my frustration, the heat of my anger, the enormity of my fear and most of all the boundlessness of my love. I poured them into Aidan and hoped he could taste them. For somebody who claimed to be a writer my words consistently failed me when it came to Aidan and my feelings for him.

When he squirmed underneath me I stopped thinking.

"I need you." God did I need him after the emotional overload I'd just been through. I longed for him to take me hard.

"Make me."

I kissed him again while my hands got busy pulling his shirt out of his trousers. As soon as I had his upper body naked, I explored it with my mouth. I teased him with my teeth and tongue until he squirmed underneath me. I angled my body so our hard cocks rubbed against each other. Desire flowed through my veins, goosebumps erupted on my skin and a sense of power I'd never experienced before made me lightheaded as I continued to drive myself and Aidan crazy.

We established a rhythm for our grinding groins. Partially clothed it shouldn't have felt as good as it did but I could feel the pressure building. I didn't need a lot more stimulation before I'd come and judging by Aidan's noises he felt much the same.

I stilled my movements and shifted my weight, keeping Aidan still below me. His dark eyes were almost black, his lips swollen and his breath came in gasps.

"Don't stop. Whatever you do." The desperation I heard in his voice matched the one I felt in my groin.

"No intention to." Full sentences became too much of an effort. I opened his trousers and crawled back while I pulled them off him, making sure to take his boxer shorts in the same movement. His cock glistened at me. Our frotting had spread a thin layer of pre-cum across the tip, tempting me to clean him. I said a silent prayer of thanks that he'd taken his shoes and socks off earlier.

I crawled back up along his legs, kissing and nibbling as I went. I contemplated teasing him when my mouth reached his groin but my own impatience was too strong for games. I licked his balls before sucking one of them into my mouth. Aidan bucked against me. I felt his hand on my head, solid but gentle. The slight but immovable pressure of his hand told me, he'd no intention of allowing me to stop.

I sucked and licked and reveled in the noises he made and the small but uncontrolled movements of his hips. I switched balls and heard Aidan's rising need in his voice. I wished I had two mouths when I reluctantly released his ball and licked my way up his cock. It trembled under my tongue and the rush of power that gave me added another notch to my own desire.

I loved the salty taste of him and took the tip of his cock in my mouth, sucking and licking it, making sure not a drop of the precious pre-cum was wasted. The tension in his legs told me Aidan tried to hold back. I wanted him frantic and sucked harder until he couldn't stop himself from bucking and pushing more of his cock into my mouth. I surrendered to the rhythm he set and took him deeper on every invasion. When I accepted all of him without gagging for the first time since we'd gotten together both of us stilled for a moment, before I slowly released his cock.

"Grab the lube and a condom." I hardly recognized my voice as I ordered him to do my bidding.

His eyes darkened further. As he turned to the bedside cabinet I crawled off the bed and shed the T-shirt and boxers I'd worn, allowing them to fall where they did. I stood still, staring down at Aidan and wondered how we'd ended up in this position. I'd never been in charge before but didn't want to hand control back to him now that I had it. His heated gaze traveled up and down my body with such intensity I experienced it as a caress. When I touched my cock and stroked myself a few times he groaned. "Jaysus Lennart, you're killing me."

"I haven't even started."

Surprise flashed across Aidan's face. Neither of us had suspected this version of me existed.

"You want me to make you, do you?" I asked.

Aidan didn't take his gaze off my cock as he nodded.

"You want me to take charge, is that what you're saying?" When had I turned into a tease?

"Yes." Aidan took hold of his own cock.

"Stop." He released his cock as soon as I said the word.

"Lube." I held out my hand and waited as he squirted some of the gooey stuff on my hand before spreading it over my fingers.

"I want you to watch me without touching yourself or me." Some instinct I'd never known I possessed had taken over and I decided to follow it, wherever it might take me.

"Spread your legs." Something resembling shock appeared in Aidan's eyes and I grinned when I realized what he had to be expecting and how that differed from my plans.

As soon as he'd assumed the position I wanted him in I got back on the bed. I lay down between his spread legs, my head close to his feet and my feet on both sides of his upper body. I moved myself around until my arse rested just above his groin, I didn't want to hurt or squash his cock over the next few minutes but I did want him to have the best possible view. I placed most of my weight on my head and pushed my hand between my legs, my middle finger pressing against my arsehole.

"Oh man." The words escaped Aidan on a breathless whisper.

I'm not sure who got teased more as I pushed my finger past the muscles and inside my body. I wished I had a way of seeing Aidan's face and decided then and there I'd have to invest in a mirror for the ceiling. The noises he made as I stretched myself were louder than those I made myself. I felt a slight movement in his body and reminded him. "No touching."

"You're killing me." I heard no resentment in Aidan's voice, just heat and lust. His hands closed around my ankles, as if he had to give himself something to hold on to because I wouldn't allow him to touch either himself or me in any sexual way.

I took my time and allowed myself to fully enjoy all the sensations. I'd never done this before but rather than feeling awkward about exposing myself to Aidan in such a shameless way, I felt empowered and in charge. If Aidan had been prepping me he couldn't have driven me crazier than I did myself. When I pushed a second finger in with the first one my breathing became ragged and my cock leaked pre-cum on my stomach.

"I wanna touch you. Please let me touch you." The combination of heat and pleading in Aidan's voice pushed my lust even higher.

"No. I'm in charge, remember?" I had to catch my breath before I could continue. "You watch while I drive you crazy."

He groaned and moved his lower body until the stem of his cock nestled in the top end of my arse crack but didn't move his hands.

I hadn't known finger fucking myself while Aidan watched would be this hot. My desire to have him inside me made me contemplate taking him there and then but the last bit of common sense left in my head stopped me from doing anything rash. I pushed a third finger in and relished the self-inflicted burning sensation. I moved my hand harder, spread my fingers and forced myself to continue preparing my hole until the burning sensation faded and only pleasure and need remained. When I felt the tension building in my balls I withdrew my fingers and moved off Aidan.

Crawling over his body I kissed and bit him wherever my mouth landed. His eyes were heavy lidded and he gazed at me as if he'd never seen me before.

"You liked that?"

"Yes... So hot." He could barely say the words.

"What do you want? Tell me."

I would have given him anything he asked. Even if meant topping him.

"I need to be inside you. Please."

A rush of excitement ran through my body when I heard the need in his voice. A sadistic streak I hadn't known I possessed made me ignore his plea and take his mouth in a long and demanding kiss first.

"But I'm in charge." I saw in his eyes I'd come close to teasing him as far as he could go. If I wanted to stay on top — in more ways than one — I couldn't wait much longer.

"Please. Please." He pleaded with me again but I saw his muscles tense as if he was preparing to take over.

"Put that condom on." Aidan's fingers were clumsy in his haste and he cursed his way through ripping the package open and pushing the protection over his throbbing cock. As soon as he was ready I hovered my ass over his crotch and positioned the tip of his dick against my entrance.

The stretch burned as it always did when he first entered me. No amount of preparation could take that sensation away, and for the first time I realized I wanted it that way. The pain before the intense and mind blowing pleasure made this experience more potent, allowed me to feel closer to Aidan.

I took my time both to tease him and to allow my body to adjust. I never took my gaze off Aidan's face as his cock slowly disappeared deeper into my body. His gaze was fixed on the point where our bodies would soon be touching.

I rested for a moment when all of Aidan was deep inside me, giving myself the time to get used to him and to marvel at the fact I'd taken charge. For a moment Aidan just lay there, looking at me in wonder. Then he bucked his hips, his patience disappearing in the heat of the moment.

I moved with him and kept going. I forced myself to go slow as I moved my body up and down. I wanted to imprint all of this on my mind. I didn't know if this would turn out to be a one off or something we'd explore more often. I never wanted to forget what Aidan looked like beneath me, his mouth open, his breathing ragged and his eyes filled with love and lust.

"More. Harder." Aidan's voice had lost its pleading quality. I might still be on top, but I had no doubt who had just taken charge. Since his demands mirrored my own needs I'd no problem complying.

I rode us until the muscles in my thighs burned from the exertion and still I didn't stop. Need screamed in my body but I told myself to wait just a little longer. Aidan had less patience than I did and his hand wrapped around my cock. He stroked me in time with my movements and it wasn't long before I could feel the tension in my balls reach the point of no return.

"Yes. Oh God, yes." I roared out the words as my orgasm hit me. My body tensed around Aidan's cock and I tried to keep on moving while my body jerked and spasmed.

My eyes wanted to close but I forced myself to look at Aidan's face. His expression betrayed how close he was, the frantic movement of his hips confirming that impression. I wanted to imprint the man who wouldn't walk away from me despite the risks, on my brain.

"Love. Yes." His cock expanded in my arse and despite the condom I felt his semen as it jerked out of his cock.

Only when his body relaxed again did I allow my eyes to close and my body to slump down on his. I wrapped my arms around him and pulled him as close as I could despite the sticky mess between us.

"Never ever do that again." Aidan's voice was soft but the words were made of steel. "Being in a relationship means we handle shit together. If you don't want to be in a relationship anymore you can tell me to leave. As long as you love me and I love you we're a partnership."

I opened my eyes and saw a face filled with love and determination below me. Until that moment I hadn't fully realized exactly what I'd been about to do. The enormity of what living without Aidan would mean hit me like a ton of bricks.

"I won't. I promise. I'd rather be homeless with you than live here on my own." The words escaped my mouth without any thought and were the truest thing I had ever said.

Chapter Twenty-Four

My arms hurt by the time I made it back to our street and I once again cursed how easily I got distracted these days. I'd had every intention of getting the shopping done early in the day. I'd decided to do some writing first and lost myself in the story. When I heard Aidan's key in the door we still didn't have any food in the house.

"Working in the dark again?" He'd laughed, not at all bothered that I'd not gone shopping and there was no sign of food appearing on the table anytime soon. "I'll go with you to the shops, just give me a minute to drink a glass of water first."

"No, you stay here and relax. I know you—you're dying for a shower. It's not your fault I get too distracted when I write. Relax. I'll get what we need. It won't take me long."

Of course it had taken me longer than I'd hoped to get home with the groceries. There'd been no taxis outside the supermarket when I'd come out with four big bags stuffed to the gills. By the time I reached our street my arms were aching.

I sighed with relief now that I could see the end of my journey. I had dinner planned in my head. I'd boil the spinach and ricotta pasta and serve it with hot olive oil and parmesan. My mouth watered just thinking about it. I'd picked us up a nice bottle of white as well.

I got so caught up in my plans for dinner I nearly missed the signs.

The door stood wide open. I stopped walking and looked up and down the street while wondering why Aidan would have gone out and why the hell he hadn't shut the door behind him. A few cars drove up and down the street but I saw no other signs of life. A black car with a Mayo license plate and a 2013 registration was illegally parked in front of our house.

My body knew before my mind did. Dread crept up my spine and a cold sweat broke out on my forehead. I crept closer to the front door and carefully pushed the shopping bags inside.

I held my breath while I listened. At first I didn't hear a sound, which worried me more than loud noises would have done. Aidan always had music on when he was home. The silence felt like a living, breathing presence, reaching out to capture me in its tentacles and strangle me.

Something fell and shattered inside and I heard a muffled curse.

"Keep him still. Jesus, he's not that big. What good are you if you can't control a kid like him?"

Dread turned into a deep and familiar fear. The sound of his voice alone was enough to send me hurling toward panic. His words paralyzed me. My father was inside my house with at least one other person and they had Aidan.

My mind flew back ten days. We'd gone to the garda station together and reported the letters and the threat.

I'd also confessed that I had recognized our attackers and told them about my recent memories of what they'd said before they ran away. I'd sat through a severe telling off and a speech about withholding evidence before they took our statements as well as the proof we'd brought and told us they'd investigate.

When over a week had passed without any news and no further contact from my father, I'd allowed myself to relax. I should have known better.

A shout and what sounded like a slap pulled me out of my stupor. I pulled my phone from my pocket and called nine-nine-nine. I told them what I'd found, what I knew and what I suspected and also gave them the name of the garda who'd taken our statement. The conversation seemed to take forever.

When I finished talking, the operator told me not to go inside and to keep the line open. I had every intention of following those instructions. I didn't want to go inside and confront my father. My heart beat hard enough to hurt my ribcage and I had to count to stop myself from hyperventilating. I leaned against the wall next to the front door and tried to calm myself down when I heard another slap.

"Now tell me where the little brat is or we'll do some serious damage." The vehemence and hate in my father's voice stunned me.

"Kiss my…" The sound of a blow cut Aidan's sentence off and turned his words into a shout.

Something snapped inside me. My feet moved without a conscious thought on my part. I walked into the house and listened. Soft groans came from the first floor. I looked around and saw the hurl in the corner next to the coat rack. I picked it up and silently crept up the stairs.

Calmness settled on me. All fear and panic had disappeared. I had only one goal, to get my father away from my lover. I didn't care how.

"Aaaahh." The sound of Aidan in pain transformed the calm into a dark rage.

The scene I saw when I stopped on the threshold of our bedroom nearly broke my resolve. A big hulk of a man I'd never seen before stood behind Aidan and held him tight in an arm lock. My father stood in front of a completely naked Aidan who bled from his nose and had a cut next to his eye.

"Just tell me where the little prick is and this will stop." My father's voice sounded almost seductive.

"No." Aidan's voice was hoarse and soft and yet he sounded determined and sure of himself.

When my father raised his arm I'd had enough.

"Looking for me?"

He dropped his arm and turned at the sound of my voice. "There's the little faggot."

The contempt in his eyes no longer hurt me. I couldn't remember why I'd ever wished this despicable man would accept me.

"Lennart, no! Go away. Get help. Go, please, just go."

The pleading note in Aidan's voice tore at my heart but I didn't take my gaze off my father as I ignored my lover's request.

"You're trespassing. You should go." I didn't recognize the ice cold tone in my own voice. Shock flashed across my father's face before his all too familiar sneer reappeared.

"Or else? You're gonna stop me? You and what army? I know you. You're a little coward." He took a step toward me and continued, "You'll be running before I'm halfway across this room. Do what your fuck buddy tells you to do and run like the spineless weakling you are."

I tightened and loosened my grip on the hurl in a rhythmic motion. I wouldn't attack my father, I didn't want to lower myself to his level but I couldn't help hoping he'd come for me. I wanted an excuse to hit him over the head so badly I could taste it.

I could hear a voice coming from my phone. I'd left it on the ledge next to the bedroom door, the connection to the operator still open. I couldn't quite hear the words but knew they'd be telling me not to confront him. Well, for what it's worth, I didn't. I stood still and waited for my father's next move. If I could just keep his attention diverted from Aidan until help arrived…

He took a few more steps in my direction.

"You can end this, you know." He'd changed his voice. In the past this trick had always worked on me. He'd go from angry to apparently reasonable and out of sheer relief I would agree to whatever he'd suggest. "You sign the deeds to this house over to me and you'll never have to see me again." Disgust crept into his voice. "Or me you."

The whole situation felt surreal to me. I couldn't for the life of me remember why I'd been so afraid of him or how he'd been able to indoctrinate me for so long.

"Like Aidan said. No."

Again I shocked him. He looked at me as if he'd never seen me before, and I guess he hadn't. Even I hadn't known this Lennart existed.

"You owe me this house. I've sacrificed enough for you. My big plans postponed by nineteen years because I had to look after you."

I stared at my father in wonder. "What are you talking about? You never sacrificed anything. When you weren't shouting at me you ignored my existence. Where's the sacrifice in that?"

"I had to look after you, didn't I? It's not as if your mother was there to care for you."

Only a moment ago I'd thought he couldn't hurt me anymore and now his words cut through me like a knife. "It's not my fault she died."

I stared at him as he opened his mouth, silently daring him to blame me for that as well, if only because it would allow me to turn the pain back into rage, but he closed his mouth again and for a moment the angry lines disappeared from my father's face.

"No. That had nothing to do with you." His frown returned. "But that doesn't change the fact I was saddled with you — the child I'd never wanted in the first place."

"What?"

"Your mother wanted a child and I..." A sad smile transformed my father's features into a face I couldn't remember ever having seen before. "I could never refuse her anything." He shook his head and glared at me. "And then she died, leaving me stuck with you. And you had to turn out just like your grandfather. All you've ever been is a reminder of everything that's wrong in my life. The wife I loved and lost, the father who betrayed me and the memory of my mother. But it stops here. You don't get to hurt or hold me back anymore. You'll sign this house over to me because I've more than earned it."

I shook my head. "This is my house. My grandfather wanted me to have it because you treated him like shit and kept him away from me." I still sounded like a stranger to myself. "What is it you used to say? You make your decisions and then you live with the consequences. I guess you don't like it when you have to live with the consequences of your own actions." I sneered at him and registered the uncertainty in my father's eyes with satisfaction. His gaze dropped from my face to the hand holding the hurl.

"If you attack me, he" — he pointed at the giant still holding Aidan — "will break your boyfriend's neck."

I glanced at my father's accomplice for a moment and noticed his grip on Aidan had loosened some. He didn't look nearly as aggressive or sure of himself as he had a few minutes ago, either.

"I've no intention of attacking you." My voice and my gaze were steady. "I just want you and your assistant" — I smirked when I said the word — "to leave. Now."

"Not without the deeds." A trace of desperation had crept into my father's voice.

I heard sirens approaching and nearly smiled. Nobody else paid the sound any attention but then, only I knew their destination.

"First of all, I don't have them here." I told the truth. After my father's first letter we'd decided it would be better to keep the paperwork in the lawyer's safe rather than the drawer in my desk. "But even if I did, I'd still have no intention of handing them over to you."

The sirens were closer now and I could hear tires screeching around the corner.

"What the fuck?"

Fear flashed across my father's face before it transformed into pure rage.

"You little bollix…" He rushed toward me and raised his hand. I counted his steps while I tightened the grip on my hurl. My father pulled his fist back and…

"I wouldn't if I were you, sir."

I'm not sure who resented that voice more, my father or me. I'd stood there waiting for him to hit out at me so I could use my hurl. Even with the garda behind me, and more people rushing up the stairs, it took all my restraint not to use the weapon in my hands.

I didn't turn to look at Aidan until a uniformed guard grabbed my father. The giant who'd been holding Aidan had surrendered without any sign of resistance. Aidan stood unaided but only just. He swayed on his feet and even from a few meters away I could tell he could barely focus on me.

I reached him and held him up before I realized I'd started moving.

"Can you walk?"

"Pobaby."

I looked at his face and saw the bruise and swelling on his cheek. Anger erupted in me again and I glared at my father.

I brought Aidan to the bed and helped him lie down and get comfortable.

"Sir?"

I looked away from Aidan and stared at the garda.

"The paramedics should be here in a few minutes. We're taking the suspects away now. We'll need your statement some time tomorrow but I understand the whole incident has been recorded so it shouldn't take too much time."

I barely managed to nod at him before returning my attention to Aidan.

"See? I was right." He winced as he tried to smile.

"About what?" I knew exactly what he meant but he deserved the pleasure of pointing it out to me, of rubbing it in.

"You can't walk away from us anymore than I can."

I smiled, then kissed him. Because—as always—he was right.

Epilogue

Nine months later

"Are you going to open that?"

I looked up at Aidan and saw a huge grin on his face. "You've only been staring at it for about fifteen minutes."

I drew the moment out. It was a first, and a huge one. I wanted to make the feeling last as long as I possibly could.

"If you don't open it, I will. I want to see what it looks like up close. I want to touch it."

I shook my head and smiled at Aidan, unsure which of the two of us was more excited.

After a few more minutes, I took scissors to the package and slowly opened it. My heart stuttered when I looked at the contents. In my hands I held ten copies of my book. I still couldn't believe this was real. It had been a mad few months. Between finishing the book, having it accepted by a publisher and going through the whole editing and cover design process, this moment felt like I'd at last stepped off the rollercoaster. Another one of my dreams had come true.

Aidan picked one copy up and turned it in his hands before opening the book. I watched him closely and knew exactly when his eyes caught them, the few sentences in the book he hadn't proofread for me. When he looked at me I was sure his eyes were more watery than they usually were.

"Oh man." He looked at the page again and read the lines out loud. *To Aidan, for recognizing what I was too blind to see and for sticking around when the world fell apart. You have my heart. Forever.*

I'd never seen him as cute and bashful. He grinned, wiped at his eyes and grinned some more before leaning over and kissing me. "And you have mine."

I nodded, able to accept his words at last. For the longest time I'd refused to believe he would stay. A small part of me waited for the moment he would come to his senses and leave. He never did. Not even when I tried my hardest to make him go.

Our lives had been good since the whole affair with my father ended. He never got a jail sentence, but that's Ireland for you. People got convicted for not paying their television license regularly, while those with money and influence, got away with probation only. I'd become enraged when my solicitor first told me the news but I'd learned to live with the fact.

I let it go. My father didn't deserve my time and energy anymore. I'd resigned myself to the fact this rift would never heal. Aidan told me not to be too hasty in that decision but how do you forgive a father who would rather have you dead than see you live in the house he wanted to claim for himself? The decision to cast him out of my life had been easier than I expected. The time had come to concentrate on my own life and the future, leaving the past and my father where they belonged, behind me.

"Much as I could look at this all day" — the silly grin had returned to his face — "we have a room to finish before Connor arrives." Aidan looked at the book in his hands again before closing it and putting it on the table. "I can't believe you did that. I love you."

His kiss was hot and soft at the same time. He wasn't starting something, not trying to get me hot and bothered — although my cock did stir, as it invariably did when we were close — just letting me know how much I meant to him.

When Aidan ended the kiss I got up and grabbed his hand. "Yes, let's get the painting done so your little brother doesn't have to sleep in fumes when he arrives." Aidan's now eighteen-year-old brother was about to start college. We'd decided to repaint the room I'd made blue for Aidan. After living together for more than a year we knew he wouldn't have any need for it.

Connor almost didn't make it into third-level education. His parents were in no position to help him out financially and a grant would cover either rent or food and drink. Connor could have found himself a part-time job like a lot of students did, and spend the next four years balancing work with study. I told him that life's too short.

I looked forward to Connor moving in with us. When my father told me he'd never wanted me, he'd severed whatever tied us together. I'd left my past, my father and any regret about our non-relationship behind me. With Aidan I'd started a new life, his family had welcomed me with open arms and I'd learned a valuable lesson. We are born into our blood families for better or worse. Families of the heart on the other hand, are those we create with the people who truly love us.

I'd been lucky enough to have been given the chance to build such a family for myself, and I embraced the opportunity with open arms.

About the Author

Helena Stone can't remember a life before words and reading. After growing up in a household where no holiday or festivity was complete without at least one new book, it's hardly surprising she now owns more books than shelf space while her Kindle is about to explode.

The urge to write came as a surprise. The realisation that people might enjoy her words was a shock to say the least. Now that the writing bug has well and truly taken hold, Helena can no longer imagine not sharing the characters in her head and heart with the rest of the world.

Having left the hustle and bustle of Amsterdam for the peace and quiet of the Irish Country side she divides her time between reading, writing, long and often wet walks with the dog, her part-time job in a library, a grown-up daughter and her ever loving and patient husband.

Helena Stone loves to hear from readers. You can find her contact information, website and author biography at http://www.pride-publishing.com